TWEEN FICTION EL

THE CAT AT THE WALL

THE CAT AT THE WALL

DEBORAH ELLIS

Groundwood Books
House of Anansi Press
Toronto / Berkeley

Excerpts from "Desiderata" from *The Poems of Max Ehrmann*, Crescendo
Publishing Company, Boston, 1948, p.83.

Published in Canada and the USA in 2014 by Groundwood Books

Groundwood Books / House of Anansi Press
110 Spadina Avenue, Suite 801, Toronto, Ontario M5V 2K4
or c/o Publishers Group West
1700 Fourth Street, Berkeley, CA 94710

We acknowledge for their financial support of our publishing program the
Canada Council for the Arts, the Government of Canada through the Canada
Book Fund (CBF) and the Ontario Arts Council.

 Canada Council Conseil des Arts
for the Arts du Canada

 **ONTARIO ARTS COUNCIL
CONSEIL DES ARTS DE L'ONTARIO**

Library and Archives Canada Cataloguing in Publication
Ellis, Deborah, author
The cat at the wall / written by Deborah Ellis.

Issued in print and electronic formats.
ISBN 978-1-55498-707-8 (pbk.).—ISBN 978-1-55498-491-6 (bound).—
ISBN 978-1-55498-492-3 (html)
I. Title.
PS8559.L5494C38 2014   jC813'.54   C2014-900974-7
                                              C2014-900975-5

Cover illustration by JooHee Yoon
Design by Michael Solomon

Printed and bound in Canada

MIX
Paper from
responsible sources
FSC® C016245

To those who bring kindness to chaos

One

___

MY NAME is still Clare.

That much is the same, although no one calls me Clare anymore.

No one calls me anything anymore.

I died when I was thirteen and came back as a cat.

A stray cat in a strange place, very far from home.

One moment I was walking out of my middle school in Bethlehem, Pennsylvania. Then there was a period of darkness, like being asleep. When I woke up, I was in Bethlehem — the real one. And I was a cat.

I don't know if it was an accident, like some sort of cosmic wires getting crossed, or if God is playing a joke on me or if this is all a nightmare and I'm really in a coma back in St. Luke's Hospital.

Nobody has told me anything.

But I went to Sunday school for as long as my grandmother was alive, and I never heard of anything like this in all their tales of heaven and hell.

Something happened a few days ago. I can't stop thinking about it, and I'm not used to thinking very much about things.

It started off with me sitting on the Big Wall.

This wall looks a little like the ones that go beside freeways to cut down the noise and to keep drunks and idiots out of traffic, although the wall here is bigger and runs through neighborhoods. There are guard towers here and there, and in some places the wall is shorter but has more barbed wire on top.

I spend a lot of time sitting on top of that wall. I like to look down on people. From the top I can look down on people on both sides. They don't do anything all that interesting, but it helps to kill time.

As a cat without a television, I have a lot of time to kill.

The other night I was on the edge of a village, not far from Bethlehem city. The night was one of the dark ones. No moon. Stars not much help. The darkness was no problem for one side of the wall, where lights shone bright in the windows. On the other side of the wall it was all dark. The power over there was not working. The only lights shining on that side were the spotlights from the watch towers, and they mostly shone down on the wall. They made the graffiti bright, but everything else looked darker.

I was sitting on the wall after getting away from a bit of a mess that had happened on the ground a couple of hours before. I was getting hungry and dropped to the dark side of the wall to find something to eat.

The darkness didn't bother me. Since I became a cat, my eyes see better in the dark than they did when I was a girl. My nose works better, too, which is not always a good thing. The world is a very smelly place.

I went looking for something to eat in the long stretch of weeds that runs along the wall. I've been a cat for a while, maybe a year, but I'm still not any good at catching mice, and I stay far away from the rats. That leaves handouts, garbage and whatever I'm fast enough to steal.

The weeds were full of garbage. Bags and bags of it, most of them torn open. I went up to each one and sniffed it, hoping to find a bit of kebab or chicken. I wasn't coming up with much, just whiffs of what had once been there. Any food had already been eaten by the other cats.

Greedy cats. They never leave me anything.

There were cats all through those weeds that night, hiding among the trash and bedded down in the tall grass. Their smells were all part of the general stink I had to sort through.

I didn't realize I was in the king tom's territory until I saw his giant head loom up from behind a clump of clover. The spotlight from the tower made a halo around his ears.

I froze. He froze. We stared at each other, still as statues.

For a second I hoped that he might let me pass. After all, I'm very scrawny, no threat to him at all. Attacking me would not be very much of an accomplishment. I even thought he might take pity on me.

But there was a hiss and a yowl, and then I started to run.

He came after me. I ran faster.

He was bigger but I was scared. I ran and I kept running.

Our running disturbed the other cats. I stepped right on top of some of them. Others were hit by boards or tin cans I knocked over as I ran. They joined in the chase, and soon I had a whole pack of cats running after me.

I don't know what they would have done if they'd caught me. They probably didn't know, either. Cats aren't great planners. I don't think they would have killed me, but they could have hurt me pretty bad, teeth and claws being what they are. There were lots of cats around with one ear or no tail or missing an eye.

If I got injured, who would take care of me? Nobody. I'd be in pain and all alone.

So I kept running.

I swerved suddenly off the grass and down a narrow street into the village. The cats kept chasing me. We ran around corners and over the tops of cars. I scrambled up to the flat roof of one of the little houses and was able to pause for a breath before the pack found me again.

Run, run, run. Up one hill and down another. It's all hills in that area. I prayed that the cats who were chasing me would get bored and stop. But they didn't.

At the top of one hill, not quite as high as some of the others, I saw a little house. It stood beside a vacant lot full of rocks, weeds and more garbage.

Two soldiers in full battle gear were at the door, trying to get in.

They were being quiet about it. No shouting or banging, like soldiers sometimes do. Just pushing and shoving. The door wasn't budging.

I ran toward them, thinking they might give me some sort of protection.

The gang of cats was getting closer. I was getting really tired.

The soldiers pushed at the door. It would not open.

The cat behind me yowled. It was right at my heels, and the soldiers in the doorway still seemed very far away.

I was on the edge of giving up and letting the cats get me. After all, I already died once. The first death turned me into a cat. The next might turn me back into a girl.

But I put out one final burst of energy.

At the same moment, the soldiers gave the door one great push.

The door opened. In the breath of a second I dashed through the soldiers' legs and scooted into the dark, low space under a sofa.

I heard the soldiers enter the house and close the door behind them.

I was safe.

Two

Or was I?

I did a quick sniff-scan to see what else was in the house. No other cats, no dogs. Just humans. And where there were humans, there was bound to be food.

I inched up to the front of the sofa to watch what was going on.

The two soldiers moved quietly, placing their duffel bags gently on the floor and walking with silent boots around the house. It was one of those one-room houses. I'd sat in the windows of others, looking in and begging for table scraps.

The house was tidy. So tidy that I could see at one glance there was not much that would interest me. There was a shelf full of books in Arabic, a bed off to one side, a little table with three chairs, and the sofa that was my hiding place. A low window had a sill that would be wide enough for me to sit on if I felt like doing that. On top of a shelf lay a violin and a bow, gathering dust without a case. My music teacher would have had a fit. He was always on us about taking proper care of our instruments. They weren't even ours — we just borrowed them from the school for the year — but he went on and on about it.

There wasn't much more than that in the little house. A couple of cupboards, a couple of low tables, a few cushions. Nothing matched, and the walls probably hadn't been painted since Jesus was born.

The kitchen was just a kerosene stove, a small sink and a shelf with a few dishes. I noticed an old coffee jar holding dried chickpeas. There were some little jars of spices, a box of tea and a couple of onions that had sprouted.

Not much of value to a little cat.

Beams of light from the soldiers' flashlights swept like brooms into the corners and along the walls. They looked behind curtains and inside the tiny bathroom.

"There's nobody here," I heard a soldier whisper.

"Good. I don't want to deal with them."

"They don't want to deal with you, either, Private."

The other soldier put his finger to his lips. He tiptoed across the rug to a pile of boxes along one wall. When he got there, he suddenly kicked out, scattering them and pointing his rifle at the debris.

"Come out! Hands up!" he shout-whispered in Arabic.

Nobody appeared.

"Big man, Private Simcha. You've just destroyed some kid's art project."

He shone his flashlight on a note-paper sign taped to the wall.

"I don't read Arab," Simcha said. "Can't speak it, either, except for *Come out! Hands up!*"

"Arabic, not Arab. It says City of Dreams."

I stuck my head out from the bottom of the sofa to get a better look at what they were talking about.

Against one wall, spread out and arranged in an orderly fashion where it hadn't been kicked apart, was a toy city built from trash. Biscuit and salt boxes had been made over into houses and shops with cut-out windows and doors. Tin cans were set on top of the boxes to look like water tanks on rooftops.

"City of Junk is more like it, Aaron." Simcha kicked out at the boxes again.

"That's Commander to you," Aaron said. "Don't trash the place. We may be stuck here for a few days."

"We're supposed to be thorough."

"We're supposed to use our brains," said Aaron.

Then he suddenly dropped to his knees and shone his flashlight under my sofa. The light was bright in my eyes.

I hissed and swiped out at him, then dashed to the back of the sofa, out of reach against the wall.

Aaron jumped. He cried out and dropped his flashlight. I smelled blood.

Got him! I smiled.

I never knew before all this that cats can smile. But we can.

Simcha clicked his rifle. He repeated his Arabic phrases. "Come out, hands up!"

"Relax," said Aaron. "It's just a cat."

"A cat? The way you jumped, I thought it was a terrorist."

"I didn't jump," Aaron said, which was a full on lie because he full on did.

"This will be easier without the family here," said Simcha. "It must be kind of awkward to take over a house that people are living in."

"Stop talking so much," Aaron ordered. He lowered himself to the sofa, then rose right up again, as if he remembered that I, Killer Cat of the Middle East, was lurking beneath, ready to strike. That's what I told myself, anyway. Like I said, I'm a cat without a TV. I have to entertain myself any way I can.

Aaron knelt down on the carpet, took a map out of his pocket and unfolded it on the floor. He shone his flashlight down on it. I wiggled to the front of the sofa to watch.

"We were here," he said, pointing with his finger. "Then we went up here and turned right here, down through Shepherds' Field." He moved his finger on the map as he talked.

"What's wrong?" Simcha asked. "Are we lost?"

"I said be quiet." Aaron continued to stare at the map.

He had my sympathy. It's easy to get lost in this place. Small streets, tiny lanes that twist and turn and have no names, hills that all look alike.

Aaron looked from the map to the window, trying to figure out which direction it faced.

"It must be the right house," he said, more to himself than to the other soldier. "A house on a hill next to a vacant lot, east of the refugee camp, south of Bethlehem. This must be it. It should give us a good vantage point."

"We've seen nothing *but* houses on hills," said Simcha. "But what do I know? I'm fresh off the boat from America. You were born here."

"I was born in downtown Tel Aviv," Aaron said. "You think I hang out in the Territories? My last post was Jenin. This might as well be the moon."

He took out a little pocket voice recorder, pressed a button and spoke quietly into it.

"Unit 37 entered the home at 4:15 a.m. As far as we know we have not been detected by the neighbors. The residents of the home are not in as we begin our surveillance of the community. All is quiet."

He clicked off and put the recorder back in his pocket.

Simcha bent down and opened his duffel bag. My ears perked up. I hoped they were about to have breakfast.

"I don't see what you're so worried about," Simcha said as he reached into his bag. "There are no wrong

houses here. These people are always up to something."
He pulled a tripod stand out of the bag and set it up by
the window.

"Yeah, like raising their families, going to school and
minding their own business. You Americans come over
here and join the IDF and think it's the Wild West. It's
not that simple."

"You don't know me at all," Simcha said.

Aaron stood at the window, even though it was way
too dark to see anything.

"We'll know at first light if this house will work. It
should give us a good view of the neighborhood. If not,
we'll radio in and get further instructions."

Simcha attached a telescope to the tripod. "All I'm
saying is that if we catch a terrorist, the brass won't care
if it's the terrorist we were supposed to catch or another
one. Either way, we'll be heroes."

"Just what the world needs," Aaron said. "More
dumb-luck heroes." He moved two chairs over to the
window by the telescope. "It's not about catching terrorists. It's about keeping people safe."

"Us or them?"

"On a good day, both."

"You sound like my parents. All you need is love …"
Simcha sat on the chair in front of the telescope. He
lowered the tripod so they could spy on the neighbors
without having to stand up.

The windows were already draped with lace-type

curtains. Aaron arranged the curtains over the telescope, hiding it from the outside view.

My ears started to itch.

Fleas. I hate fleas.

I never got lice when I was in school, not even in the fourth grade when almost every other kid in the class was sent home to get the nits picked out of their hair.

Crawlers, I used to call them. The kids, not the lice. "Here comes another Creepy Crawler," I would say, pointing and laughing at the kids with the lice.

I never once became a Crawler myself.

It's not right that I should escape lice when I was a girl but have to deal with fleas now that I'm a cat. People who have lice when they're alive should be the ones to get fleas in the afterlife because they already know how to deal with them. Fleas to them would be no big deal.

That's just my opinion.

I tried to twist my body so that I could bring up one of my hind legs for a good scratch, but the sofa was too low. There wasn't enough room. I rubbed my ears on the carpet. That helped a bit, but not much.

I could feel myself sliding into one of my frustration fits. Well, who wouldn't, in my situation? It was all so unfair! Bad enough to be dead at thirteen, but then to come back as a stray cat in this awful place, full of rocks and shooting and ridiculous heat and way too many other cats.

If I had to come back as a cat, why couldn't I be like my sister Polly's cat? Ty-kitty was fed roast beef from the table and snoozed on the sofa all day, waking up only to eat and watch TV. I wouldn't have minded that so much.

I absolutely needed to scratch, and I wanted to get away from the carpet, which stank of cigarettes and tear gas. I wanted to move to a higher place where I could breathe in less-smelly air, be out of the reach of the soldiers and keep a good eye on whatever was going on.

But I wanted to eat more than I wanted to scratch. If I was up high and they brought out some food, I might not get down in time to snatch it away.

If they decided to eat.

And if they dropped any food.

I didn't know how long I'd have to wait for food, and I hate waiting. I never liked it. And there was so much waiting around when I was a girl! Waiting for the Monopoly game to end so I could escape from Family Game Night. Waiting for my father's client to finish his will-writing appointment so that I could watch TV in the study instead of in the rec room with my sister. Waiting for my mother to get off the phone and drive me to the Westgate Mall.

I hated all of it. My heart would start to pound and I'd want to wring someone's neck.

"It's not good for me to have to wait," I told my parents. "Really, it isn't healthy. I'm not kidding."

But they just went on making dinner or mowing the lawn or talking on the phone to Grandma, even though it would have taken them No Time to do what I wanted.

I wonder if they're sorry now.

Sometimes I was able to get what I wanted by being really, really bratty about it. I'd unplug the lawnmower or I'd stand right in front of my mother while she yakked on the phone.

"If I drive you this one time will you promise to settle down and not act like this again?"

Of course I promised. And of course I did it again.

Now I either wait or I go do something else. And nobody cares. It's terrible. Nobody ever thinks about the wants and feelings of a stray cat.

I rubbed my ears on the smelly carpet again, then closed my eyes. Cats can nap anywhere.

My ears perked up at the sound of a package being opened. My nose twitched. I smelled cheese. One of the soldiers had unwrapped a hunk of cheese and was cutting it into pieces.

In a flash I was out from under the sofa. I grabbed a big piece of cheese and bounded up to the top of a cupboard.

"Hey!"

I held the cheese in my teeth and raised my hind leg to my ear and gave those fleas a good hard scratch. It felt like heaven.

I scratched, then I ate. The cheese stuck in my throat a bit, but I didn't care.

Simcha, laughing, reached out to grab the rest of the cheese. I hissed and swiped at him, scratching his hand.

He stopped laughing and backed off.

Now both of them were scratched. I wasn't a bit sorry.

When my breakfast was done, I enjoyed a long session of grooming. I've learned that grooming my fur is as soothing as brushing my hair used to be when I was a girl. I used to love brushing it and looking at the shine of it in the bathroom mirror, no matter how often it made my mom late for work. I don't think that's vanity, to admire something beautiful, even if the beautiful thing was me.

I had another good scratch. Then I settled down on my perch for a nap. I was feeling so good I almost decided to purr.

Then my nose told me something I hadn't paid attention to before.

There were three humans in the little house.

Two of them were the soldiers.

The third was a boy. And he was hiding.

Three

WHAT DID I care if a boy wanted to hide? It had nothing to do with me.

The best thing about being a cat is that nothing is my fault.

Oh, I suppose if I deliberately ran in front of someone carrying a huge tray of bread rolls on his head, making him trip so the rolls went flying into the gift shops along the narrow streets of old Bethlehem, that would be my fault. (And has been, more than once!) But no one would ever blame me in a serious way. No one would think to punish a cat. No one would bother giving a detention to a cat.

I've become a living Get Out of Jail Free card.

So what if a boy was hiding? So what if the soldiers had taken over his house?

So what if he might be in trouble?

Not my fault. Not my problem.

I reminded myself of this when I sniffed out the boy.

Not your business, I told myself. You have enough trouble of your own, stuck in this awful place with fleas and no TV. That boy hiding away will never help you. So why should you help him?"

That got my thinking straightened around to where it should be, back to the place where most of my thoughts and feelings have been since I died.

On hatred for my homeroom teacher.

She was the one responsible for my death. That means that all the stuff that's happened to me since is her fault, too.

She had it in for me from the start.

She was new to Lehigh Middle School. I came back from summer vacation expecting to have Mr. Hutchins for eighth grade. He told jokes in his class and was so close to retirement he didn't care what his students did as long as they were quiet about it. But over the summer he went and had a heart attack, ruining my plans for an easy school year. He was out, and this new teacher was in.

I walked into her classroom on the first day of school just five seconds late and she practically ripped my head off.

She didn't say anything. She just looked at me with ice-cold eyes. She didn't even respond to my smile, a smile that most adults thought was sincere.

I sized her up right away — forty, frustrated, forgettable, a long way from young and a long way from retirement. Her hair was in tight, short poodle curls edged with gray. She wore a drab navy dress that made her look more like a cop than a teacher.

I thought about staring her down but instead flashed another of my winning smiles to show she hadn't gotten to me and took a seat at the back of the room. I liked to sit at the back because I could see everything from there. I needed to stay on top of things so I'd know who to make fun of.

"My name is Ms. Sealand," this new teacher said. "I will be your homeroom teacher and I will also teach you history and literature."

I texted my impressions of Ms. Sealand to my friend Josie, stuck in the other eighth grade class in the school. I kept my eyes on the teacher while I texted. My grades were good. As long as I pretended to pay attention, teachers usually left me alone.

Ms. Sealand babbled on about the usual start-of-the-year stuff. I didn't listen. I was busy texting possible nicknames for her. *Sealand* made me think of seals and walruses, but they didn't quite fit. *Sea* also sounded like *Zee*, and then I had it. Zero. We would call her Ms. Zero.

"Is everyone happy with their seats?" the teacher asked. "Anyone want to change? This is your one and only chance."

I smiled at the comment Josie texted back about Ms. Zero.

"Good," the teacher said. "Everyone, please pick up your desks and pivot them one hundred and eighty degrees."

I had a vague sense of the confusion around me as the other kids tried to figure out if she was serious. But Josie was texting the nickname of her teacher, so I didn't take much notice of anything else.

My phone was snatched out of my hands.

"Hey!"

The word came out of my mouth before I could stop it. When dealing with teachers, the first rule is to look like you are on their side. Any outright expression of disagreement is the sort of thing they remember, and you don't want them to remember the bad stuff.

The teacher stood silently at the back of the room, which was now the front of the room. She had four cellphones in her hands. One of them was mine.

I suddenly realized I was the only kid who hadn't turned her desk around. I felt stupid doing it while everyone was watching, and especially stupid because Ms. Zero waited in silence until I was done.

"You have all been informed of the school board's no-phone policy," she said. "If you would like to change that policy, you are welcome to follow the democratic process and make a deputation at a meeting of the board."

"Do we get our phones back at the end of the day?" someone asked.

"Your parents are welcome at any time to come to the school and retrieve them."

I tried my smile again. "My mother likes to know that she can get in touch with me."

"Then perhaps you could share the school's general phone number with your mother," Ms. Zero said. "Before we begin our lesson, let me say a few other things. This school year will be unlike any school year you have had to date. I believe in respect — giving and getting. You all have my respect from the start because you have shown up today, ready to learn. My respect for you as individuals will grow or wane throughout the year. You choose which by your attitude and your behavior. I am not your friend. I am not your parent. I am your teacher, and I put a high value on that. It is a value I hope you will come to share. If so, I can promise you will leave this classroom in awe of the power of your own minds."

She went on and on about how it was our job to keep up with her, not her job to chase after us, that assignments turned in late would get a zero unless we had prior clearance from her, and that she would be conducting regular sessions on time-management at lunch hour.

"These sessions are open to the entire school," she said. "There is a sign-up sheet by the door. I suggest you sign up early."

Then she handed out a Statement of Agreement. We each got three copies.

"This is a contract between you and me," she said. "It clearly states my rules and expectations, and it also outlines what we will be studying together and what the major assignments will be. You and your parents will sign all three copies, as will I. One copy is for your parents, one is for me, and the last one is for you to keep. I enjoy clarity in communication. The world provides enough ambiguity."

"She can't make us sign this," I whispered to the girl across from me. I was a lawyers' kid. I knew a little bit about contracts.

"You have an objection, Clare?" Zero asked.

"No one can be forced to sign a contract," I said. "What if we don't want to sign?"

"You and your parents are welcome to meet with me to discuss your objections."

She had an answer for everything.

There was no way I was going to show that contract to my parents, but I wasn't worried. I was good at forging their signatures.

"Let me be clear," the teacher said. "Next year you will be in high school. A very few short years after that, you will legally be adults. This year is to prepare you for that. It is time to grow up."

And then she smiled. It was like a smile on a vampire.

"We will also have fun. You will find that school is much more fun when you are treated like mature students instead of like little children who need to be babysat. And the fun part begins now. Human beings tell each other stories to try to bring order to chaos. What do I mean by that?"

All the bright-eyed kids jumped into the discussion. I used the time to come up with a story for my parents about losing my phone. They had made me promise not to bring it to school.

"Allahu Akbar."

The call to prayer interrupted my thoughts. It was loud. The mosque must have been close to the little house I was hiding in.

"Ashhadu an la ilaha illa Allah. I bear witness that there is no God except one God."

Another day was starting.

Another bloody day.

Terrific.

Four

————

I DISCOVERED that I can now understand all the languages humans speak.

This is how I figured it out. I was in downtown Bethlehem, in the square outside the church that now stands on the spot where Jesus was born. There were a lot of tourists eating lunch and dropping bits of food. Someone left half a burger on their plate while they had their picture taken — plenty of time for me to help myself!

I wandered among the legs of all the people in cafes and eating ice cream in Manger Square. Many were in organized tour groups, with guides carrying the flag of France or Japan or India. There were women in saris, men in multi-colored African shirts and women with black kerchiefs on their heads. There were Muslim women in head coverings and Greek holy men in long black robes.

It was pretty clear that people were there from all over the world. I heard all their conversations, and I wondered why everyone was speaking English.

Then I realized that they weren't, but that I could understand them anyway.

At first it was pretty cool, and I wandered around, listening to people talk and feeling pretty pleased with myself that I could understand everything. I could eavesdrop on *everybody*!

Then it dawned on me that a lot of what I was hearing was really boring.

"Where's the bathroom?" "Did you see what they charge for a Coke?" "Is this really where Jesus was born, or are they just guessing?" "If this is how you are going to behave, next time we'll leave you home and your Aunt Alice can watch you." "There's only so much junk we can pack in the carry-on, and I'm not paying extra for shipping, so get that in your head right now." "Many beautiful Holy Land souvenirs, right this way." "Are there toilets over there?"

I understand the animals, too, just as clearly as if they were speaking English. They're not any more interesting. They mostly talk about food and the stupid things humans are doing. Dogs on leashes talk about wanting to run away. Cats think they're better than everybody, so they make fun of everything. Except the birds. The birds make fun of the cats. If they are fast enough.

Not a single one of them, human or animal, has ever even bothered to ask me how I am doing and if they can do anything to help me. All selfish. All of them.

Anyway, I figured out, with no help from anyone, that there are only two languages — human and animal. The difference between the two is that animals can't lie. Or don't. Really, they have no reason to lie. Humans wouldn't hear them and other animals wouldn't believe it. Which is too bad for me because lying is the thing I was best at when I was a girl.

So when the two soldiers talked in Hebrew, I could understand them. And when the people out in the street spoke Arabic, I could understand them, too.

I can only make cat noises, though. In my head I'm saying words, but it comes out of my mouth as meows.

Daylight was beginning to replace the darkness. Aaron spoke occasional updates of "All quiet" into his little voice recorder. The soldiers went through their duffel bags and spread their things out as they settled into the house. I watched them closely.

I like Things. I did when I was a girl and I still do now that I am a cat.

I was a pretty good little thief when I was a kid. I kept a shoebox in the back of my closet of little things I stole — an eraser from one classmate, a ruler from another, a red marking pen from the teacher's desk, my sister's favorite My Little Pony, a brooch from my mother's jewelry box, a Pittsburg Penguins hockey puck my father kept on his desk in the den. Later I took things of more value, like a watch out of someone's gym

bag in the school change room, a set of pastels from the art class, and any money I could get my hands on.

I spent the money, of course, but I kept the Things. I liked to look through my treasure box in the middle of the night when I couldn't sleep. I thought about people looking for their things and not being able to find them because I had them. It made me feel powerful.

I guess someone probably went through my closet after I died and found the box. My family should have kept my room the way it was and turned it into a sort of shrine to me. But my mother was way too practical. She probably moved Polly in there and turned Polly's room into a study for herself so she could work at home without having to share space with my father.

I hope it was Polly who found my box of Things. I wasn't very nice to her, but she would never rat on me, not even after I was dead.

All this is making me sound like I was a really bad person, but I wasn't. There were a ton of things I could have stolen but didn't. And I wasn't always mean to Polly. Sometimes we would listen outside the door of my father's study while he helped a client write a will and we would hear who would get what. That was fun, and I was nice to her then.

One time we listened in on the parents of one of the boys in my class. They were asking my dad about dividing their estate. "Our daughter is a star but we don't think our boy will amount to much," they said. "Do we have to leave them the same amount?"

I never told that boy what I heard. I could have. But I didn't, because I knew it would hurt him. So I wasn't all bad. I think I was pretty normal, actually.

When the two soldiers opened their bags and started sorting through their stuff, I decided to go down to the floor for a closer look, to see if there was anything I might want.

I got right inside one of the bags and shoved things around with my nose, looking for something I liked. It was a little bit like shopping.

"Hey, kitty! Look, kitty's in the duffel bag!"

I let the soldier called Aaron run his fingers through the fur on the back of my neck for a moment. I even decided to purr.

"She likes me," Aaron said. "Who's a pretty cat?"

"That is the ugliest cat I have ever seen," Simcha said. "And this land is full of ugly cats."

"Don't pay any attention to him, Miss Kitty," Aaron said in a baby-talk voice. "I think you are the prettiest kitty. Really, you are. My mother would feed you up and have you looking sleek and fine in no time."

I heard footsteps outside. The two soldiers jumped to their posts, one at the telescope and one at his rifle.

The town was awake.

Five

___

I SMELLED sage. I could tell from the rhythm of the footfalls that the passerby was an old woman heading down to the market with herbs to sell for making tea.

The soldiers kept their guard up. Aaron quietly recorded everything he saw out on the streets, all the comings and goings of young moms and old men. They also kept their backs to me, so I took the opportunity to keep shopping in their duffel bags.

I poked around their belongings, looking for something small enough to carry away. Among the socks and ready-to-eat meals I spied a packet of gummi bears. I almost took them. They reminded me of my old life. But they were wedged under an ammunition clip and I couldn't get them out.

I decided to take a small pack of batteries. I dragged it under the sofa and lay down on top of it.

Mine.

There. I felt better.

There are little stashes of things I've stolen all over this area, on both sides of the Big Wall. I wish I could keep it all with me.

A package of batteries is not very comfortable to lie on, so I left it and went back out to sniff around some more.

I wandered away from the duffel bags and over to the pile of trash called the City of Dreams. It *was* trash — boxes, bottles and tin cans spread out over the entire end of the room. Unfortunately, at first sniff it seemed like it was all spotlessly clean, without a speck of food in any of it. The boxes had been cut and reassembled to look like houses, churches, schools, things like that. There were bridges made from toilet rolls and a castle with a drawbridge. Stop signs were made out of sucker sticks and red bottle caps. Toy cars and little army men dotted the streets along with tiny crocheted dogs, birds and mice. There was even a park with trees and benches.

Someone had worked hard on it. If it was a project for school, some kid was bound to get an A.

I kept sniffing.

I could smell the boy. He was hiding in the middle of the cardboard city. He was sweaty and scared and hadn't washed in a while. He had wet himself, too. All his smells were making it very hard for me to tell if there was any food around.

He was having trouble breathing. I could hear it because I have fantastic hearing now. The soldiers couldn't hear it because they were paying attention to the street. They kept up a whispered conversation.

"I'll bet you there's a terrorist in that house with the ivy growing up the side," said Simcha.

"That's not ivy. It's sweet pea. Or honeysuckle," Aaron said.

"Honeysuckle? Why would terrorists be growing honeysuckle?"

"You think terrorists would be more likely to grow ivy than honeysuckle? That makes no sense."

Their argument was completely pointless and I tuned them out as much as I could. I settled down near the head part of the buried boy. I looked closely at the area and saw how he had managed to hide.

The City of Dreams was built over a trap door. The soldiers couldn't see it because there wasn't much light in the house, but I could. Most of the toy houses were loose on the floor. Some had been glued down over the trap door to disguise it. All the banging on the door the soldiers did when they were trying to get into the house must have alerted the boy and given him time to hide.

I noticed two things, then, almost at the same time.

One was an inhaler, the kind people with asthma use. It had rolled under a low table and was in a shadow next to a table leg.

The other was that the boy's breathing had gotten much worse. Whatever oxygen was in that little hiding place, he was using it up fast. His noises reminded me of Colin, a kid with asthma who got locked in the art-supply cupboard in the second grade.

I already said that it was none of my business if a boy wanted to hide, and I believed that.

But when I heard him breathing like little Colin, I decided I should do something.

It took me a while to figure out what, because I'm not used to doing things for other people.

While I was thinking, the boy's breathing got worse and worse, until finally I just started to howl.

I meowed and screeched and dug furiously at the trap door with my paws, scattering the loose cardboard buildings and making a great big fuss.

The soldiers finally shut up and tried to get me to be quiet. They threw things at me — socks, the packet of gummi bears — but I stayed where I was and kept doing what I was doing.

Finally, one of the soldiers came over. That's when he heard the boy's labored breathing and wheezing.

"Someone's here!"

The two of them found the hidden door, yanked it open and lifted the boy out of his hiding place. They dropped him face down in the City of Dreams. One soldier pulled his hands behind his back and the other pointed a rifle at his head.

Six

———

NEXT CAME a lot of shouting in whispers.

"Who are you? Why are you hiding? Where is the rest of the family? Who left you here on your own? What is your name?"

The soldiers asked the same questions over and over, their guns pointed right at the boy's head. They blindfolded him and placed him so that he was sitting cross-legged facing the wall. His hands were cuffed behind his back.

"Who are you? Where are the others?"

The boy was having too much trouble breathing to answer. Being out of the hiding place and in the room where there was more air probably helped, but he still needed his medicine.

I kept waiting for the soldiers to figure out what was wrong with the boy. But they were too busy interrogating him.

The boy was seven or eight years old and very skinny. He wore cheap jeans that were filthy and too short and a long-sleeved red T-shirt with a rip in the shoulder. He sat with his head up and back, trying to gulp for air. I could see from the way his shoulders moved that he was putting his whole little self into the struggle.

I have to do everything, I thought.

I went to the little table and batted the little inhaler until it stopped at the foot of one of the soldiers.

They were still too busy screaming at the kid, so I raised myself up, found a spot on one of them above his boot, dug my claws in and bit him on the leg, right through his uniform trousers.

Then I zoomed back under the sofa to watch the fun.

The soldier I bit — who turned out to be Aaron — spat out a string of curses and pawed through the duffel bag for the first-aid kit. Simcha finally noticed the inhaler.

"Kid — is this yours?"

But he asked in Hebrew, which the kid apparently couldn't understand because he didn't answer. Plus, he was blindfolded, so he couldn't see what the soldier was holding in front of his face.

"Aaron, do you know how to work one of these things?"

Aaron looked over. "My brother uses one. Shake it first. Does that cat look like it has rabies?"

"Ten giant needles, right into your stomach, Commander," Simcha said. He shook the inhaler, read the instructions, held it up to the kid's face and gave the boy a dose.

The boy breathed easier after that.

The quiet seemed to calm the soldiers down. Simcha did another search of the little house, which involved scattering the City of Dreams all over the floor. Aaron took a sudden intake of breath at the sting of the alcohol swab on the bite wound. He seemed like a nice guy. I probably shouldn't have bit him quite so hard.

"Seven a.m.," Aaron said into his recorder. "Discovered male child, primary school age, hiding in false floor. Child can't or won't account for himself. Location and identity of his parents is unknown."

I rubbed my whiskers against Aaron's boot to show there were no hard feelings. He patted me gently, then patched up his wound. The two soldiers took up their posts again by the window, one with the rifle, one with the telescope.

The fleas were still bothering me. I spied the boy's hands tethered behind his back with plastic twist-tie handcuffs.

I went up to him, meowed a couple of times so he'd know I was a cat and not a rat, then positioned myself so that his fingers were at my ears. I bumped my head against his hands, just so he got the message.

As he got busy scratching the flea zones, he calmed down. He'd been crying a bit but eased off, and then he stopped altogether. I started to purr — for real, not just for show.

It was a very peaceful scene. Through the window

the sky changed from dark gray to silver to a rainbow of sunrise colors. I've seen so many sunrises since I became a cat, more than I ever saw as a human. But this one was special. The colors made the two soldiers look even younger, almost as though they could have been classmates of mine.

I had a sudden memory of my mother, coming into the kitchen from the yard in the summer, fresh-cut flowers in her hands, dew on the petals and dew on her. I paid no attention to it then.

People and flowers are freshest in the morning.

Cats? We've usually been up all night, roaming around. By the morning we look grizzled and done.

I purred and purred and felt my whole body relax.

And then I heard the boy start to whisper.

It was very faint, barely a whisper of a whisper. The soldiers probably couldn't hear it. But I could. And I didn't like it.

I tried to ignore it.

The words got into my brain anyway.

He was speaking in Arabic, which, as I've said, I can understand now.

I thought I was having a nightmare. I moved away from his hands and climbed into his lap to hear better. I still didn't want to believe what I was hearing so I put my front paws on his chest and raised myself up so that my ear was right next to his mouth.

"Go placidly amid the noise and the haste …"

I stood there and listened to him recite the whole damn poem. When he got to the end, he started again at the beginning. He spoke the poem as if it were just one long word.

There was no mistaking what he was saying.

He was reciting the Desiderata.

He was reciting the punishment poem.

Seven

"THERE ARE many theories of punishment," Ms. Zero said.

"There is the belief that punishment should be retribution, that it should make the offender suffer," she continued. "Others believe that the main purpose of punishment should be to help the victim feel better. Should a punishment be so terrible that it deters others from committing the same crime? Is punishment ever a deterrent or do offenders always believe they will get away with their crime?

"We are going to talk a lot about this in the coming months because you will soon be in a position to make decisions about these things. For example, if we put someone to death for killing someone else, does that make us killers, too? I can see that a lot of you have things to say about that, and I promise that we will have that discussion another day, probably over the course of many days as you try to come to terms with the world you are inheriting. But for now, let's talk about detention."

She took a rolled-up poster off her desk and held it in front of us.

"Your Statement of Agreement already lays out the consequences for infractions such as tardiness and the incompletion of assignments. Detention in my class is something different. Detention will be given out in response to acts of meanness — bullying, unkind behavior and actions that are disrespectful of others."

She asked two students up to the front to unroll the poster so everyone could see what was on it. It was a poem. A long one.

"This poem is called 'Desiderata.' It was written in 1927 by Max Ehrmann. Who would like to read it out for us?"

Several of the Bright Eyes shot their hands in the air. One of them went to the front and started reading.

"Go placidly amid the noise and the haste, and remember what peace there may be in silence ..."

The poem went on and on.

I hated it from the beginning.

It sounded like something my grandmother would say. "Look for the good in people, Clare-bear," she would say as we peeled potatoes together in the church soup kitchen. "If you look for it, I guarantee you will find it."

She was crazy.

And the punishment poem was stupid.

"Be yourself ..." Bright Eyes read. *"With all its sham, drudgery and broken dreams, it is still a beautiful world.... Strive to be happy."*

It was probably the longest poem in the history of poems.

"Copying out this poem will do two things for you," Ms. Zero said. "The act of sitting still and copying will give you a chance to calm yourself and perhaps reflect on your own actions. And the words of the poem will challenge you to think about who you are and who you want to be. So this is what will happen. The first detention, you will copy the poem once. If you get a second detention, you will copy the poem twice. You see where I'm going with this?"

She smiled and some of the class laughed. It didn't concern me. I never got detention. All the teachers loved me.

"You can do the work at recess or after school," she continued. "Or, if you have several copies to do, you can do them at home. Handwritten copies only, all legible, all complete. It must be on my desk by the start of school the next day. If it isn't, one more copy will be added to your detention for each day it is not completed."

Like I said, I never got detention. I was pretty and got good grades and was always careful to treat the teachers with respect, at least to their faces. I flew under the radar.

The teachers all wrote nice things on my report cards, but my grades weren't so spectacular that they singled me out as some sort of leader or something. The teachers were happy, my parents were happy, I was happy.

Toward the end of the second week in Ms. Zero's class, I got my first-ever detention.

We were all in the gym for a guest speaker because the auditorium floors were being waxed. I hated having assembly in the gym. We had to sit on the floor like little kids, in straight rows, legs crossed, teachers sitting on chairs around the sides of the room like jail guards. Just like the soldiers who sit in the towers on top of the Big Wall, looking down on the people in the village. Just like me when I sit on the wall.

The theme for the school year was "Reaching Beyond Our Borders." A bunch of assemblies spread out through the year were supposed to inspire us to get involved in the world beyond our school, or something dumb like that.

At the first assembly, this woman talked about poor kids around the world.

Her voice was kind of halting. I didn't know if she was nervous or if she didn't know her topic well enough or what, but it drove me crazy and I just wanted it to be over.

"I can make her freak out," I whispered to Josie. My whole crew was sitting together, as far away as possible from the Untouchables.

"Don't be mean," Josie said, but I knew she was daring me.

It was all very simple. Mostly I just smiled. I looked right at this children's rights woman and smiled through her entire speech. Not a real smile. The sort of smile my mother called a smirk.

Sometimes I would raise my eyes a bit, as if I was laughing at some hair sticking straight up out of her head.

Sometimes my eyes would go to her shoes, and I'd pretend to whisper to Josie, all the time smiling as if something was hysterically funny.

It worked. I knew it would. I'd done the same thing in church when I was bored, to supply teachers I didn't like, and to soccer coaches, too, just for fun.

The speaker raised her hand to smooth down her hair. Then she looked down at her shoes to see if one was untied. And she lost her place in her speech.

"According to UNICEF, there are seventy-seven thousand children around the world who are not in school … no, I mean seventy-seven million …"

She had to look through her notes, and she knocked them off the podium. They flew across the gym floor. A couple of the Bright Eyes helped her gather them up, but she had to take a moment to put them in order and then find her place again.

The rest of her speech was a mess. The students started to fidget and even the teachers stopped paying attention. She finished in a rush and hardly anyone applauded.

"See?" I said to Josie.

"You're not very nice," she said, but I could tell she was impressed.

Back in the classroom, Ms. Zero stood at the front of the room and was silent for a long time, even after we took our seats and got settled.

No one had been given a detention yet.

Then she said, in a quiet voice, "Clare, please write your name on the side board."

I didn't quite know what was coming, but I had a bad feeling that I was in trouble. I wanted to protest, but that would have gone against my practice of not appearing to disagree with teachers. I went over to the chalkboard as if it was a regular everyday thing, but my heart was beating fast.

"Beside your name, put a multiplication sign, then the number one."

I did that.

"On my desk, by the start of class tomorrow morning."

That was all she said.

I hung back at lunch time, feeling the need to at least pretend I didn't know why I was being punished.

She didn't even wait for me to speak.

"Your behavior in the assembly was disgraceful. I have nothing more I want to say to you right now, and there is certainly nothing I want to hear from you."

She didn't even give me a chance to talk. Like I said, she hated me from the start.

I stayed in after school to make the copy. I almost didn't. I almost left when everyone else did, but at the last minute, I decided to get it over with.

"I'll be right out," I said to my crew.

They went off together down the hall, talking and laughing and having a good time without me.

I counted the verses in the stupid poem. Seventeen. I slogged through it.

If you compare yourself with others, you may become vain or bitter, for always there will be greater and lesser persons than yourself.

On and on it went.

Ms. Zero worked at her desk the entire time I did the detention. She didn't speak to me and I didn't speak to her.

Finally I copied out the last two lines: *With all its sham, drudgery and broken dreams, it is still a beautiful world. Be cheerful. Strive to be happy.*

I handed my work in to Ms. Zero.

"Thank you," she said.

She didn't even look at me. She didn't even ask me if I'd learned anything.

My crew was gone by the time I got outside. I was late getting home. I told my father I'd stayed behind to help the remedial class. He said he couldn't ask for a better daughter.

Strive to be happy, I thought, as I flopped down on my bed. I'd be happy if I never had anything to do with that damned Desiderata again.

And now I had to hear that same stupid poem coming out of that stupid little boy in the handcuffs.

It was not very nice. It was not very nice at all.

Eight

——

I HISSED right into the boy's face to try to get him to shut up.

He kept on going. He didn't miss a word.

I jumped onto the top of his head and balanced there.

I could feel him wince from the pain but he didn't stop. In fact, he started reciting louder.

"... *everywhere life is full of heroism* ..."

And then he made it worse by starting to rock back and forth. I clung to the top of his head and howled.

"That's one crazy cat," Simcha said.

"It's hurting the kid," said Aaron. "Get it off him."

"*You* get it off him."

The boy's hair was long, curly and matted down with sweat and dust. As Aaron grabbed hold of me to lift me off, my claws became tangled in the boy's hair. Aaron held me up and Simcha had to put down his rifle to free my legs one at a time.

It was not very dignified, and I was not happy about it. I swatted out at them once they put me on the floor, but by then they had backed away. I pawed at the air like a fool and they laughed at me. I hate being laughed at. I scampered off to a corner to groom myself into feeling better.

"Is he bleeding? Are you bleeding, kid?" Aaron looked at the boy's head. "I don't think he's bleeding."

The kid rocked and recited.

"What's he saying?" asked Simcha. "Is he saying prayers? It sounds like the prayers they say, you know, before they blow themselves up."

"He's not going to blow himself up. He doesn't have a bomb on him. We searched him, remember?"

The two men stood over the boy while he rocked and whispered.

"My Arabic's not great," Aaron said. "I think he said Many fears come from being tired and lonely."

"Why would he say that?"

"I think there's something wrong with him," Aaron said. "Look at the way he's rocking. There's a kid in my little brother's class who does the same thing."

Aaron knelt down and took off the boy's blindfold.

"I don't think you're supposed to do that," said Simcha.

"We're supposed to treat the family well," Aaron said. "This house isn't under suspicion. We're just borrowing it to watch the house that is." He balled up the strip of cloth that had covered the boy's eyes and tossed it on the floor.

"Hey, kid," Aaron said gently. "Did the cat hurt you?"

The kid kept reciting the poem.

"Look how his eyes are unfocussed," Aaron said.

"It's a trick," Simcha said.

"I don't think so," said Aaron. "The kid in my brother's class was just like this."

He stood up and took a Swiss Army knife out of his pocket. He went around to the boy's back and cut through the plastic handcuffs.

"If this goes bad, I'm not sticking up for you," Simcha told him. He sat back down at the telescope. Aaron sat down with his rifle.

The boy scurried like a scorpion over to the ruins of the City of Dreams. He looked it over almost like he was a cat, peering at every piece, going from a bare spot that used to hold a cardboard building to the spot on the floor where the building had been tossed. It looked like he was drawing a map in his head of what needed doing and deciding how to bring it all together.

Then he scurried around the room, again like a scorpion that was dashing from one shady spot to the next. He gathered up all the parts of his trash city, then concentrated on putting everything back where it belonged.

When everything was placed in just the right spot, he started to make his repairs. One by one, he picked each little building up, straightened something here, refolded something there.

The City of Dreams had a lot of these tiny structures. Going through it would keep him busy for a while.

He seemed a lot happier. Well, who wouldn't be, to have their blindfold and handcuffs taken off? All I cared about was that I didn't have to hear that poem anymore.

"See anything sinister?" Aaron asked.

Simcha looked through the telescope. "I see an old woman in a rocking chair."

"What's she doing?"

"Rocking," Simcha said. "And knitting."

"Knitting?"

"Yeah. I never thought of them knitting. My mother knits. My grandmother, too."

"My father knits," Aaron said.

"Your father?"

"He was with ZAKA, the group that cleans up after a bombing. When I was a kid, before the wall got built, it seemed like every day there was a bomb going off somewhere. Dad went out at all hours to go pick up body parts off the street. After a while he couldn't eat his soup without his hands shaking. My mom started him knitting to calm him down."

"Did it work?"

"Yeah. He makes beautiful things."

The two of them yakked on and on about knitting

and favorite sweaters and a scarf one's girlfriend knitted him when he went off to training camp in the Golan Heights. On and on it went, and I could not shut it out of my brain.

If I didn't understand Hebrew, their conversation could have just been background noise that would have allowed me to slide into a lovely sleep. But instead, they got me thinking about the sweaters I used to have, the ones I liked and the ones I didn't like, and how I had to learn to knit in Brownies but couldn't do it. I made my mom do it for me so I could get the badge.

That got me thinking about piecing together quilts out of old clothes with my grandmother to give to the homeless people who slept on the floor of the church basement. That led me to thinking about the crafts table at the Christmas bazaar and how one lady always made these dolls with crocheted dresses and big skirts that draped over the spare roll of toilet paper in the bathroom.

And then I realized that I needed to go to the bathroom.

One of the perks of being a stray cat is that I can usually take care of that business anywhere I want. I generally look for a place that's kind of sheltered but has a good vantage point so I can keep watch around me.

But now I was inside this little house.

I suppose I could have gone in a corner. I didn't want to do something so personal in front of the soldiers. I knew they would just see me as a cat, but still.

I could have scratched at the door until they let me out. But I didn't think they would let me back inside again.

And I wanted to hang around for a while.

Partly because sooner or later, someone would bring out more food.

Partly because I liked being inside again, surrounded by walls, safe and cozy. Outside, the morning was quiet so far, but the riots would probably start up again that afternoon. I was tired of trying to figure out which way they would go so that I could go the opposite way. Riots have a nasty habit of changing course, and tear gas gets carried on any old breeze.

But mostly it was because I was beginning to feel like the four of us were a family — a strange family, but not much stranger than a lot of other families out there.

And I missed being with a family.

So I didn't want to leave the house.

That left the bathroom.

The door to the tiny bathroom was not latched. I gave it a push and it opened.

I was lucky that the toilet had no seat cover. I hopped right up on the seat, found my balance and got down to it.

"Well, will you look at this! Commander, come and see this cat!"

The two soldiers stood in the doorway and gaped at me.

"Who taught you to do that, Miss Kitty?" Aaron crooned.

Simcha complained about not having his cellphone to take a video.

And me?

I was caught in the middle of a very private moment, with nowhere to go and no way to hide.

I was caught by the soldiers the same way my sister Polly was caught by me and my crew after school one day. My parents weren't home yet. We waited until she went into the john, then we pushed open the door and stood there and laughed at her.

I went back under the sofa as soon as I could.

I didn't want anybody to see me.

Nine

———

I WENT to the back of the sofa, against the wall, so I didn't have to look at any of them. I could still hear them, though. The boy moved around the room, putting his cardboard city back together. The soldiers sat in their chairs by the window and talked about stupid pet tricks they'd seen on television.

The day moved slowly.

Every now and then I heard the footsteps of people going by. Once I heard a donkey. No one stopped outside the little house. No one knocked at the door.

"What's this kid doing here all by himself?" Simcha asked. "Where are his parents? What's wrong with these people?"

"His parents must have thought they'd be back soon," Aaron said. "Maybe something went wrong."

"Are you on their side, then?" Simcha asked. "I thought you were the one whose father cleaned up bodies after bombings."

"Yeah, well, this kid didn't do any bombings."

"Not yet," said Simcha.

"Do you think he's hungry?" Aaron asked. "Kids are always hungry."

At the mention of food, I moved to where I could watch Aaron search the little kitchen. He rattled the chickpeas and touched the sprouted onion. Then he went to his duffel bag and pulled out a pack of field rations.

"You're going to feed him?" Simcha asked. "Take it out of your stash. Don't expect me to share mine."

"You'll do as you're told," Aaron said, "but I'm giving yours to the cat." And then he actually did snatch one of Simcha's ready meals. He opened it up and put it on the floor.

I pushed my face right into the chicken stew before Simcha had a chance to leave the telescope and grab it away from me.

Aaron heated up a meal for the boy with the automatic heater in the pack, then did one for himself. The boy dived into his dinner like a fish returning to water.

Aaron put Simcha's meal on the table. Before Simcha could get to it, I left mine and started eating his. I knew he wouldn't want it after I'd been in it. That way I'd get two meals.

It worked. Simcha tried to pick me up to get me off the table but I made my body go like a rock. Simcha was stronger and bigger, but I relied on the condition that affects most humans — they don't want to be cruel to animals.

"Stupid cat," he said, and left me alone to stuff myself.

"Simcha," said Aaron. "Your name means joy in Hebrew. Is that your real name or did you call yourself something else in California?

"It's my real name."

"Your parents are religious, then, to give you a Hebrew name."

"My parents are hippies," Simcha said. "I have a sister named Sunshine."

"Are they in Israel, too?"

"They're back in California. They run a surfing school for underprivileged kids. That's why I came here, to open a surfing school of my own. There's good surfing here. I'll do my compulsory military service, then spend the rest of my life on the beach. You?"

"Fifth-generation Sabra," Aaron said. "My ancestors escaped pogroms and planted orange groves in the desert."

"Cool," Simcha said.

"Yes, cool."

Cool, I thought, wishing they'd shut up. A sister named Sunshine. I wondered if Simcha ever made fun of her when they were growing up. Probably.

My sister and I were named after saints. I was named after St. Clare, who started up some nuns way back in the dark ages. Clare's not a bad name. Polly wasn't so lucky. She was named after a guy named Polycarp who hung out with the apostle John. As soon as I heard that, I started calling her Fishface.

My parents weren't religious but my mother's mother was hardcore Catholic. She even moved to a Catholic Worker House after my grandfather died. I used to help her out in the soup kitchen there every weekend. Grandma was fun to be with, even though she gave away all her money and spent all her time with homeless people who didn't dress very well.

"Serve with a joyful heart and the joy will come back to you, Clare-bear," she was always saying to me.

She was joyful to all the people who came to eat there.

Right up until one of the druggies killed her for the five dollars she had in her pocket.

Being kind doesn't lead to anything good.

The boy finished with his meal. He licked his tray clean. He took it over to the City of Dreams, got some scissors and tape off a shelf and started turning it into a new house for his city.

Aaron collected the rest of the trays, rinsed them off in the sink and gave them to the boy.

The boy reached into one of the turrets on the castle and brought out a bag of candies. He offered one to each soldier. Aaron took one. Simcha didn't.

I butted my head against the boy's leg. He handed Simcha's candy to me. I took it in my teeth and stored it away under the sofa.

Another Thing that was Mine.

"What are we going to do with him?" Simcha asked. "What if his parents don't show up and we have to leave? Do we take him with us?"

"I don't know," Aaron said. "I haven't run into this before. When we've taken over a house with a family, we put everyone in the back room. The parents look after the kids. I guess we'd have to take him with us and turn him over to the unit commander. Make the kid *his* problem."

"You look as though you don't like that plan."

"I don't," said Aaron. "I've seen full-blown riots form out of the blue on a calm sunny day. These people get some tiny bit of half-baked information and blow it all out of proportion without even bothering to find out if it's true or not. Next thing you know, someone's shouting, stones are flying, some idiot starts tossing Molotov cocktails, and people are getting hurt."

Aaron thought for a moment, then picked up the radio.

"I'm going to call it in," he said. "It's one of those little things that could turn into a big thing. Let someone higher up make the decision about what to do with the boy."

He turned the radio on. All he got was a bit of static. Then even that went quiet.

"Battery's dead," he said. "Get the spares, will you?"

Simcha looked around for the spare batteries. Then

Aaron looked. They couldn't find them because they were under the sofa where I had hidden them.

"I'm sure I packed them," said Simcha. "Can we use the recorder batteries?"

"Wrong size," Aaron said. He looked out the window. "It's quiet out there now. Maybe we should just go."

I could have handed the batteries over to them, but I didn't want to. There were more ready-to-eat meals in the duffel bags. I wasn't going to let the soldiers get away until I had another chance at a good meal.

I went to the door and plopped down in front of it, blocking their way out.

Nobody was going anywhere.

Ten

――

THE SECOND detention I got was for not moving.

I was in the hallway with my crew, standing by the long row of lockers near the autoshop room. We were doing what we usually did when we weren't in class — hanging out, eating, brushing our hair, talking about other kids and complaining about teachers. Nothing special. For sure nothing evil.

None of us had lockers in that section, but we liked to hang out there because the hallway was narrow and we could all find a locker to lean against and still look at each other and talk without having to shout. Plus we liked that all the kids coming down the hall had to pass close by us, and sometimes we wouldn't let them. Some of the boys coming out of autoshop were funny looking, and we could make them feel bad. There was also a teachers' washroom in that area. We could stare at them as they came out and make them think they had toilet paper on their shoes or something. We could see what everyone was wearing and if their hair looked funny. It was fun.

There was one kid in our school in a wheelchair. He had cerebral palsy and was really popular, even though his family had no money, he couldn't play sports and he didn't wear cool clothes. I never talked to him.

He had a motor on his wheelchair so that he could move it himself. I could see him coming toward us, and I decided I was tired of him being so popular for doing nothing more than sitting in a wheelchair. I didn't even think about it, really. I mean, I didn't plan it ahead, but when his wheelchair started to come toward me, I decided to stay where I was and not move to let him pass. I turned my back to him. I kept looking at my friends and talking, and anyone looking at us would think I didn't know the wheelchair kid was there.

I could see from the looks on my friends' faces that they could see what was going on and thought it was hilarious.

Wheelchair kid started to ask me to get out of the way, but he couldn't really speak very well, so I decided to continue to pretend he wasn't there.

He kept trying to ask me to move, until I turned around and said, "Is there something you want? Speak up!"

My friends all giggled, although they did it behind books that they held up to their mouths. I was brave enough to laugh openly. I stopped only when I saw from their eyes that something was wrong.

Ms. Zero, of course, was creeping up on us.

We wouldn't have kept Wheelchair Boy trapped for long, but did that matter to Zero? Not a bit. She just jumped to the conclusion that we were doing something wrong. No, that *I* was doing something wrong.

I stepped aside and let Chair Boy pass. I didn't even wait to be told to. I should have got some credit for that.

"Times two," she said to me, before starting a conversation with the Chair and continuing down the hallway.

When I got back to my homeroom, my name was back on the chalkboard, with a times two beside it.

At the end of the day, I stayed behind after class to write out the copies. I didn't plan on speaking to Ms. Zero. There was nothing I wanted to say to her. I just wanted to get the punishment done and get away from her.

"You'll have to do the work at home," she said. "I'm leaving now."

"I won't be long," I said.

"No, you won't be," Ms. Zero said. "You'll be leaving now, too. I have to lock up the classroom."

"I don't have a copy of the poem at home," I said.

"That's a problem," she said. "It's a good thing you have a brain that will assist you in finding a solution."

"I'll take the poster home," I decided, and moved to take it down from the bulletin board.

"That stays here," Ms. Zero said. "It belongs to me." She held the door open for me and motioned with her head that it was time for me to go through it.

"How am I supposed to do the detention?"

Ms. Zero said nothing except, "Have a good evening." She locked the door behind her and walked away from me down the hall.

So I didn't do the detention. I suppose I could have looked it up on the internet but I didn't think of that until the next morning. It wasn't my fault. It was hers for not suggesting it. But that didn't keep her from taking one look at her desk at the beginning of class the next morning, then crossing to the side chalkboard and changing the number two beside my name to a number three.

I stayed in at lunch time and copied out the stupid poem three times. Ms. Zero was having one of her time-management seminars. All the desks were taken. I had to stand the whole time.

It was completely, completely wrong. No one should ever be treated like that. She should never have been allowed to be a teacher.

Eleven

——

I WAS looking forward to a good sleep. I was full of food. I was inside a house and my back was against the door so that nothing could get me by surprise. I was going to have a real, sound sleep for a change, instead of napping with one eye open like I had to when I slept outside.

The little boy was humming while he made a new house out of the food trays. The humming bugged me but not too much. I could push it into the background and that was fine.

I was starting to drift off into a lovely sleep when the soldiers started yakking again.

"What are you doing?" Simcha asked.

"Shut up," said Aaron, which made me like him a little bit more.

"Why are you pointing the telescope up in the air? You looking for terrorists in the sky?"

"I'm looking at a Turkestan shrike," Aaron said. "At

70

least I think it is. I've never seen one before, and I don't have my book with me."

"What are you talking about?"

"My bird identification book. I'm a birder."

"A birder?"

"Israel is a major intercontinental migratory route for birds," Aaron said. "Five hundred million birds come through here twice a year. Over five hundred different species."

"Who cares?"

"Blast. It flew away."

Aaron launched into a long lecture about the importance of birds to the ecosystem, which led to Simcha talking about how surfing made him feel close to nature, and from there they moved on to talking about girls they met on the beach and on bird-watching trips.

On and on. I opened one eye and used it to glare at them, but they paid no attention.

Like I've said, no one cares about the feelings of cats.

I already knew much more than I ever wanted to know about birds. They are too fast for me to catch. Whenever I try, they fly out of my reach, perch on a branch and laugh at me.

Birds got me another detention.

Before I died, I had to suffer through my sister's school speech.

It was this thing that happened every year. All the sixth-grade kids had to give a speech in front of everyone in the school. The best ones got prizes and were entered into the city-wide public-speaking contest sponsored by the Bethlehem Chamber of Commerce.

When I was in sixth grade, we were supposed to come up with our own topic and let the teacher know weeks in advance. I figured that if I didn't give her a topic, I wouldn't have to do the speech. So, no topic.

It didn't work. One day, the teacher called my whole crew up to the front of the class, because, of course, none of us had chosen a topic. She had us draw slips of paper from Darren Brown's smelly baseball hat, then said, "These are your topics."

Mine was mineral resources of Appalachia.

I stood there, staring at it in horror, and immediately tried to swap. All my crew were against me that day. They took one look at my topic, then shoved theirs deep down in their pockets.

"You will be on that stage alone for at least three minutes," the teacher said. "I suggest you get prepared. It will be a long three minutes if you are standing there with nothing to say."

My way of getting prepared was to go to the mall with money from my mother's wallet to get a new sweater to wear on stage. As for the mineral resources of Appalachia, I just got something off the internet and read it. I didn't care what I was reading because I knew no one was listening. I got some laughs, though. They were laughing with me at how boring it all was.

When Polly got to sixth grade, she didn't choose a topic because the idea of going out in front of everyone and talking filled her with such terror that she just wanted to escape the whole thing. So she was called to the front to choose a topic from the hat.

She got birds of Pennsylvania.

Instead of fluffing it off like any normal person would do, she took her little self to the library. She stuck her face in a book. She talked on the phone with someone from the Audubon Society. She even went bird-watching at the Lehigh Gap Nature Center with the Catholic youth group. It was ridiculous.

Polly worked hard at her speech. She wrote it out on cue cards and she practiced it in her room, over and over. My bedroom was next to hers so I couldn't escape it. It made me sick the way Mom and Dad applauded when she did her speech for them after supper one night. I got so tired of hearing about the green-winged teal and the snowy plover and the nesting patterns of the pied-billed grebe.

I made plans for my revenge. My crew were happy to go along.

Polly had a big navy cardigan of my father's that she liked to wear. She could hide in it. The sweater hung on her like a potato sack and had deep pockets that she used to carry around paperback books and all kinds of junk. I knew she would keep her little cue cards in one of those pockets.

My crew and I went up to her when she filed into the auditorium with her class. We surrounded her before she could take her seat.

"Polly, good luck today!" I said, giving my sister a hug. She stood straight and stiff while I hugged her. She could tell it was phony. I didn't care. While I hugged her, I stole her cue cards out of the cardigan pocket. It was easy. I handed them off to one of my crew. We all wished her good luck and then, smiling sweetly, we went back to our seats.

Polly sat down a few rows in front of us and off to one side. I can still see the moment when she realized that her cue cards were gone. A fraction of a second later, she realized that I had taken them. She popped up out of her chair, turned around and looked right at me.

"She even looks like a carp," I said to my crew, and we all made fish faces at her.

She sank back into her seat.

When her turn came, I almost felt sorry for her. She looked so little all alone in the middle of that big stage. She stood at the microphone and didn't say a word.

"Go, Fishface!" my crew called out, just as we had planned.

The sound hit Polly like a fist. I saw her body actually buckle. Kids started to laugh.

And I truly, honestly, felt bad for a moment. I realized I had gone too far. I even thought of apologizing to her later.

But then, instead of running off the stage and putting an end to it, she unfolded herself, took a deep breath, and started babbling about the birds.

"The sun has not yet risen, but the birds are already awake. Their calls fill the air before the noise of the traffic takes over."

She spoke loudly, clearly and with such expression that I was drawn into her stupid little speech even though I had heard it five thousand times before.

She didn't need her cue cards. She knew her whole speech by heart.

When she finished, she got huge applause.

Not from me. I might have, but then she looked at me again. And this look was just rude. Defiant and rude. It was a look that said, "Screw you!"

Of course she was one of the winners. She went on to win at the ward level. She got beaten at finals, but not by much.

It got worse. A local furniture store liked her voice and hired her to record some radio commercials for them. And they paid her!

My detention came right after the speech day assembly. Ms. Zero rattled off the names of my whole gang. We all had to put our names on the board — well, mine was already there. We stayed after school to write out our punishment poems. At first it was fun because we were all there together. But I had four times more work to do than they did, and no one would wait with me while I did it. They were supposed to be my friends, and they just left me.

The soldiers kept going on and on about birds and the war and the bus stations with the best fast-food places and other things that were not the least bit interesting. Every now and then I heard the sounds of footsteps outside as people passed by. Sometimes I could smell a dog in the streets or one of those horrible cats, but mostly the world outside the house was quiet.

As the hours went by and the heat rose in the day, the talk slowed down. At some point, it trickled off altogether. The boy even stopped humming.

Then there was only the sound of the soldiers snoring and a few flies buzzing along a windowpane.

Everything and everyone else in the world was asleep.

I joined them.

Twelve

———

I WOKE up to the sound of gunshots.

I hate it when that happens.

If people insist on shooting other people, they should do it quietly so that a cat can have a decent nap.

At least the shooting was far away and did not go on and on. I could hear the low rumble of the riots off in the distance. It sounded a little like a truck and a little like thunder and a little like the crowd at a baseball game. It faded in and out with the change of the breeze.

The riots didn't happen every day. There were often weeks and weeks when things were quiet and I could look for food without worrying about getting shot or breathing in tear gas or getting hit by a rock thrown by some kid with lousy aim or getting tangled up in the feet of a hundred running people.

After a nap, I like to have a good stretch, so I did that. Then I went to see if the soldiers were ready to eat again.

They were still sleeping. So was the kid, but I didn't care about him. The kid had no food.

I was ready to eat.

I hopped up on the legs of one of the soldiers, put my paws on his chest and raised myself up. Then I screeched in his face.

"Feed me!" I screamed.

He jumped ten feet. Everyone did. I went flying. I landed okay and there was a nice bit of chaos while everyone woke up and remembered where they were and what they were doing.

"You were sleeping!" the soldiers accused each other.

The boy started to cry.

He could really wail.

"Shut him up," one soldier said to the other. "He'll draw attention to the house."

"Leave him alone. Kids cry all the time. There's nothing unusual about that."

I didn't care one way or another, but the crying and the arguing were bugging me. I like to wake up slowly, on my own time. I do as a cat and I did as a human. When I was alive I always wished my mother would wake me up by bringing me a glass of cold orange juice and quietly pulling back the curtains, easing me into the day.

"Here's an alarm clock," was what Mom said instead.

It wasn't fair, but that was my life.

Clearly, it was going to be up to me to bring some peace and quiet back to the little house, and to get everyone calmed down enough to realize they were hungry.

I went over to the crying little boy and rubbed up against his legs, purring and nudging his hands with my head, begging him to pet me. He put his arms around me. His sobs eased off, but then he started reciting the stupid punishment poem again.

The soldiers were happier, but I wasn't much further ahead.

A roar rose up from the riots.

"Hear that?" Simcha asked. "They're at it again."

"Old lady's moved," Aaron said, peering through the telescope. "She's put down her knitting and has left her chair."

"I'll alert the media," Simcha muttered.

I went up to the top shelf again to get as far away from all of them as possible. I did some grooming but my head wasn't really into it.

"It's getting late," Aaron said after a while. "It's quite late in the afternoon. If this kid has parents who left him to go to work, then they should be coming back soon."

"What happens when they do?"

"We'll let them in the house and tell them to keep quiet," Aaron said. "The boy will have his parents back and he won't be our problem anymore."

They were quiet for a while. Then, "This is really boring," Simcha said.

"What did you expect?"

"Taking over someone's house and using it as a base for spying sounded exciting when they explained it in training."

"Some homes have televisions," Aaron said. "Some of the guys in my old unit said they watched football when they took over a house during the World Cup."

"I wish we had a TV," Simcha said.

I wished we did, too. I was also bored. I decided to entertain myself by seeing if I could mess with Simcha's head.

I sat on the windowsill in front of him and groomed myself for a bit. Then I suddenly froze and stared at a spot on the wall across the room.

Simcha saw me staring. He turned his head to see what I was looking at. He didn't see anything and faced front again, trying to be cool. I kept staring at that spot, as intently as I could. I could see that my staring was bugging him. He swiveled his head a few more times before Aaron noticed.

"You got a problem with your neck?"

"That cat is staring at something."

"Seriously?"

Simcha got up to get a closer look at the wall. "What kind of weird bugs do you have here?"

"I study birds, not bugs," said Aaron. "Maybe the cat's staring at a ghost."

Simcha looked like he was actually considering this.

"The cat's messing with you," Aaron said. "It's what cats do."

I took advantage of Simcha standing to hop over and make myself comfortable on his chair. When he tried to move me off, I yowled, snapped at him with my sharp teeth and waved my claws in the air.

I didn't push my luck, though. I left the chair before he pushed me off.

Aaron broke out some more rations for everyone, although not for me. I sat by the boy and purred as he fed me bits from his meal. He laughed at the ticklish feeling of me eating out of his hand.

"I think we should leave after it gets dark," Aaron said. "Not right away, but later, after midnight. The streets will be quiet and deserted then. We shouldn't have any problems with the locals."

"You're the boss," said Simcha.

"Nothing's going on here," Aaron said. "The most interesting thing we've seen is that old lady with her knitting needles, and unless she's knitting bomb-making instructions into her doilies or whatever, then I think we can say there's nothing going on in this block."

"What about the kid?" Simcha asked.

"We'll take him with us. If no one shows up for him by the time we are ready to leave, we'll take him with us."

"If the Arabs catch us with one of their kids," Simcha said, "all of a sudden it will be that the Israeli army is kidnapping Palestinian children."

"Maybe it won't be that bad," Aaron said. "We'll just explain ourselves. Most people are reasonable. Our CO can turn the kid over to the Palestinian social services, or to some orphanage or something. They can find out about the parents and we can be done with him."

I licked up the remains of everyone's dinner. It wasn't as good as being given my own, but it was better than eating garbage.

Thirteen

———

CHRISTMAS OVER here is a big deal.

Bethlehem is not a little town. It's not anything like the Christmas carol. It's a big city with hill after hill, and it's not still at all, even though the song says it is. And the place where Jesus was born is not some little stable like you see in the nativity scenes. It's a great big church with a giant Christmas tree outside and crowds of people gathering from all over the world for an "experience."

I know all this because that's where I spent last Christmas Eve.

Christmas was a good eating time because tourists always dropped food, but there were so many people in Manger Square that a cat was taking her life in her hands dashing from one sloppy tourist to another.

It was raining that day, and chilly. By nightfall it was downright cold. I followed the crowd into the church to get warm.

It was easy to get in. There were so many people.

They had to enter the church one by one because the door was very small. People had to bend down to get through. I overheard the tour guide say that the door was called the Gate of Humility since people had to bow their heads to pass through, but really it was created by some ancient guy to keep horses or camels from getting into the church.

I wandered among the people and found some kids who wanted to pet me until their mother told them to "Get away from that stray!" I didn't care. It was good to be inside, smelling the incense and listening to the singing. It reminded me of midnight mass with my grandmother.

At the back of the church I followed the crowd down a few steep steps into a little cave-like room. It was packed with people singing and praying.

"Jesus was born right on that silver star!" a woman said to her friend. "I can't believe we are right here, right where it happened."

I squeezed through people's legs to see what she was talking about.

The silver star was embedded in the marble floor of a little nook. Curtains hung over the sides of the opening. The light was dim, so I slipped behind the curtain and hid in the little space.

No one noticed me. The parts of me that stuck out were hidden by the shadows of the candles that hovered over the star.

One by one, people knelt down at the star, touched it and said a prayer. Their faces were close to mine. Some smelled like tobacco. Some smelled like booze. Some smelled like peppermint and hot dogs.

It started to feel stuffy in there. More and more people crowded in. They were all breathing and the rain from their coats was evaporating, candles were burning and incense clouded the air.

It was all getting to be too much for a little cat.

Then I heard a clock chime the hours. I counted twelve. And when the last vibration of the twelfth chime faded away, all time stopped.

I learned in science class that this is not possible, that the world spins and the moon spins around it and therefore time cannot stop because gravity and everything else depends on it keeping going.

But time did stop.

I know this because I could see someone's watch. An old man was kneeling down beside the star. His hands were cupped over his face. I saw his wristwatch. The second hand was not moving.

I peered out from behind the curtain.

No one was singing. No one was talking. No one was even moving. Everything was still and quiet.

And that's when their souls started to talk.

I guess it was their souls. I don't know how else to explain it. No lips were moving. In fact, no one moved a muscle. They were like statues. No voices were raised.

No one was lying or complaining or asking about the bathrooms.

But they talked, just the same, all the people who were crowded into that stuffy little cave underneath the old church.

I heard them all, like a choir, their sounds swirling in the air around me. There were many voices, but they all said the same thing.

"If only I could do it again …"

Some wished they'd been nicer to their kids or their wives or their parents. Others wished they'd been braver or happier or sat in the garden more.

It's like they were all saying, *I had this precious thing and I wasted it …*

It didn't make any sense to me. They were all still alive! They had lots of time to be nice or smell the roses or whatever! I was the one who was dead. I was the only one who really had the right to have any regrets because it really was too late for me. Too late for me to be nicer to Polly. Too late for me to tell my parents I loved them. Too late for me to forget the party and go with Grandma to the soup kitchen the day she was killed so she wouldn't have been alone by the garbage bins.

As far as I was concerned, everyone in that cave was just whining and should be ashamed of themselves.

I got so mad I almost left.

But I didn't. And soon after that, the old man's watch started ticking again and everyone went back to their chattering, complaining selves. The moment was over, the songs came to an end, and the guardians of the church cleared everyone out.

I stayed. I curled up on the shelf where the baby Jesus was supposed to have been born and I thought about the Christmas detention I got.

Ms. Zero gave it out at the last minute. To this day, I don't know how she saw. It was the last class before the holidays and we were getting ready to head out of the classroom. Everyone was busy putting their stuff away and packing up their backpacks. That's when the girl in the desk beside me dropped her wallet on the floor.

She wasn't part of my crew, but she was okay. She never gave me a hard time, and when I was paired with her for a project, she did most of the work without ratting on me.

But when I saw her wallet on the floor, I didn't even think about it. I scooped it up and put it with my stuff.

A second later, Ms. Zero reached right into my backpack without even getting my permission. She pulled out the girl's wallet and handed it back to her.

To me, all she said was, "Times five."

Of course I didn't have a copy of the stupid poem at home and I was too mad to look it up. I didn't do the copies over the holidays. When I came back to class in January, Ms. Zero put a big six beside my name on the blackboard.

That's what I thought about as I sat in the spot where Jesus was born.

If I hadn't put that wallet in my bag, I would not have gotten that detention. I would not have started out the new year with so many copies of the poem to make, and I may have had a whole different time of things.

I probably would not even have died.

I sat in that spot and tried to figure out why I put that wallet in my bag instead of handing it to the girl who dropped it.

I had no idea why. I just did it without thinking.

I did it because I was used to doing things like that.

After I had that thought, I fell into a deep, satisfying sleep. I dreamed about my family on Christmas morning. My mom and dad were there, and Polly, and my grandma. They were opening their presents, and when they talked about me, they said only good things.

Fourteen

———

"It's time," said Aaron. "It's well after midnight. The streets are quiet. I think we should leave."

All their stuff was packed up. The boy and I were sitting together in the middle of the City of Dreams, watching the men and waiting.

The soldiers were nervous. Simcha kept trying the radio, hoping the dead batteries would miraculously kick back into life. Aaron kept looking at the map and muttering about the direction they came from and which direction they should go when they left.

As I've said, the Big Wall was not that far away, and once they found the wall they would be able to walk along it to one of the open places they call the checkpoints. But a lot depended on which direction they walked. The wall was hidden behind a few hills and valleys. They could easily turn the wrong way and miss it.

It was dark again, too. The power was still out. I could

see all right but it would make the journey harder for the soldiers.

I decided to go with them. It would be fun to watch them try to figure out their way back. Once they got there, they might decide that they liked having a cat around and their unit could adopt me.

"Find the boy a jacket or something," Aaron ordered. "And where are his shoes?"

The boy and I watched the soldiers rummage around for the things they thought the boy might need. The boy looked at me. I could see him thinking. He put his hand on my head and scratched my ears. I purred to reward him and to keep him doing it.

They found a jacket and put it on the boy. They put his feet into shoes and tied the laces. The soldiers picked up their rucksacks, shouldered their rifles and opened the door.

Aaron looked outside, both ways.

"I don't see anyone," he said. "Grab the boy. Let's go."

Simcha took the boy's arm. Not roughly, but solidly. They headed to the door. I was right there with them.

They got to the open door and were almost through it when the boy decided he wasn't going.

He grabbed hold of the door frame and would not let go.

He started yelling the punishment poem at the top of his lungs.

The soldiers tried to pry his hands free but he had a

grip of steel. They tried to pick him up to pull him away, but he made himself into a dead weight and would not be moved.

"Grab him! What's the matter with you? You're three times his size."

"You want me to hurt him? Is that what you want? How is that going to help get us out of here?"

It was kind of funny because the two soldiers were whispering and the little boy was bellowing. He kept it up, too. I don't think he stopped for a single breath.

They struggled with the kid for a good long moment before they retreated back inside the house.

Unfortunately, I was on the wrong side of the door when they closed it. I found myself outside.

I didn't like that at all. I was too curious to see what would happen next with these three. So I mimicked the boy. I howled. And howled.

I heard cursing from inside. Then the door opened a sliver. I dashed inside.

All that effort ruffled my fur. I groomed myself for a long time. It made me feel better.

Fifteen

———

WE SPENT the night in the little house. No parents came back for the boy. He didn't cry for them, so maybe he didn't miss them. He played in his City of Dreams, mumbling the punishment poem to himself as he picked up the cardboard houses and rearranged streets. When he got tired, he stretched out and fell asleep where he was. He was a lot like a cat.

I liked him, except for the damn poem.

Aaron lifted the sleeping boy off the floor, put him on the sofa and covered him with a blanket. The two soldiers talked quietly off and on. They took turns sleeping. It felt like a long night.

The riots started early the next day. I could hear shouts and shouting. They were closer to our neighborhood, too. Tear gas came in on the morning breeze. Everyone in the house was tense. The boy was rocking and humming his tuneless little tune, deep inside the City of Dreams. The soldiers were at the window, standing instead of sitting, rifles out and pointed.

A rush of boys came running past the house. They picked up stones and threw them almost without stopping. Aaron noted them on his voice recorder.

"They're throwing their rocks at somebody," he said to Simcha. "There must be some of our soldiers around here. We could just join them." He headed for the door. "Come on. Bring the boy. We'll leave him at a shop or something. Someone will take care of him."

"You want us to step out into a riot?" asked Simcha.

"We'll wait until we see that *our* guys are here."

But no soldiers came running after the stone-throwers, and the sounds of the riot drifted away.

The two soldiers in the house could not make up their minds what to do. They paced around, then plunked back down in the chairs by the window and glared at each other.

I went over to the boy and let him scratch my ears while we watched.

A new sound reached my ears through the babble of the soldiers.

I lifted my head and felt my ears twitch.

It was the sound of little kids. They were singing. And their voices were moving closer.

"What's that?" Simcha asked.

The sound got closer and closer until it was right outside the house.

Then it stopped. And there was a knock at the door.

I jumped. The two soldiers sprang up from their seats and backed away from the window.

"Omar!" a woman's voice called out. "Omar, are you in there? It's your teacher, Ms. Fahima."

"There's a whole pack of them out there," Aaron said.

The doorknob jiggled. Simcha took two big steps to the door and made sure the lock was on.

Omar, which seemed to be the name of the kid in the house, left the City of Dreams and went over to the door. He reached for the doorknob. Simcha pulled him away.

"Omar? Are you in there? You didn't come to school today."

The kid went back to the door to try to open it. Simcha pulled him away again.

"Help me here!" Simcha whispered to Aaron.

Aaron took the kid by the shoulders. As soon as his hands got a grip on the boy, Omar began reciting the punishment poem — loudly, as if it were all one word.

"Goplacidlyamidthenoiseandthehasteandremember…"

"Omar's home," I heard a child say.

I hopped onto one of the chairs by the window and looked out. Sixteen seven-year-olds wearing light blue school uniforms were gathered in the street.

This was a new kind of riot.

"Omar, is your mother in there?" Ms. Fahima asked. "I know she can't hear me. Could you take her to the window so she can see that your teacher is here?"

Omar kept reciting and Aaron kept holding him.

"Do something!" Simcha hissed. "Shut him up!"

"You don't give orders here," Aaron barked. He was working hard to keep hold of the squirming Omar.

Simcha found the balled-up cloth that they'd used as a blindfold and tossed it to Aaron. Aaron let it fall to the floor.

"I'm not gagging a seven-year-old," he said. "Besides, the teacher already knows he's here."

"*Speakyourtruthquietly* ..." shouted Omar.

"Omar has a kitty!" one of the children said, pointing at me. In the next instant there were sixteen little faces pressed against the window.

At first it seemed crazy. This whole place was crawling with cats, so what was so special about me? But then I kind of liked it.

I pretended I was a movie star posing on the red carpet. I rubbed my face against the glass so it looked like I was giving them kisses. They all wanted to get close to me but I wouldn't let them get too close! I pretended the glass was my army of bodyguards, keeping my many fans at a safe distance.

"Children, it is not polite to look in someone's window. Just because we are under occupation, that's no reason to forget our manners."

"Ms. Fahima, come see the kitty!" one of the little kids said.

"All right, but only to check on Omar, not to be a window-peeper."

The teacher left the door and came to the window. She bent down so she was level with me and put her face to the glass.

She came so close to me so quickly that I was startled. I screeched and arched my back like it was Hallowe'en, then jumped back and scurried under the sofa.

The children squealed with laughter.

"You made the kitty jump! Do it again!"

The teacher laughed along with them. I liked the sound of her laugh. It was not mean.

I squirmed to the front edge of the sofa and peered out.

"There's the kitty," a kid called out.

Ms. Fahima held her smile as her eyes darted around the house, looking for Omar. They widened in horror when she saw the boy held by the soldiers.

Aaron was now holding the rifle. Simcha had his hand over Omar's mouth. I don't know why he bothered. Everyone knew now that the kid was in the house.

"Do you think she's seen us?" Simcha asked.

"Of course she's seen us," said Aaron.

The teacher gathered her wits and said to the children, "Come away from the window now, boys and girls. It's such a lovely day, and there is this nice bit of yard right here. Why don't we stay outside Omar's house today and do our school work here? Who would like to do that?"

Ms. Fahima got the children away from the window

before any of them spotted the soldiers. They seemed very excited about making their school outside.

"Can we have a picnic?" I heard one of them ask.

"Very good remembering of the English word we learned yesterday! Let's all say it together."

Sixteen little voices chirped their way through a collection of English words and the alphabet song. I went back to the window to watch them.

They sat on the rocks and cement blocks that littered the yard beside the house, all of their eyes on the teacher. I couldn't see her all that well from the window. She was standing with her back to the door.

I got the message even if the soldiers didn't.

If anyone was leaving the house, they'd have to get past her.

"Nice and loud, children, so that Omar can hear us inside his house and not feel left out."

"One little, two little, three Palestinians," they sang at the top of their lungs. "Four little, five little, six Palestinians."

While the children sang, Ms. Fahima took out her cellphone. She glanced back at the house once, then turned away to watch her students.

"Who's she calling?" Simcha asked.

"Whoever it is," Aaron said, "I think we're in trouble."

Sixteen

"SHE HAS straight A's in every other class."

My mother was an assistant district attorney. She used her courtroom voice in real life whenever she was trying to get her own way. She was using it now with Ms. Zero in the parent-teacher conference.

The teacher had her own special twist on parent-teacher conferences. She thought they should include the students, which meant that I was sitting there in the classroom, my mother on one side and my father on the other. I hadn't managed to figure out a good enough lie to get myself out of it.

"She has two C's this term," my mother continued. "Both are in classes that you teach."

Ms. Zero just nodded.

"You don't have an answer?" my mother asked her.

"You didn't ask a question."

I have to admit, I liked that. Most people didn't stand up to my mother.

"Why is Clare getting C's in history and English literature? They are not hard subjects."

"She has A's in math and science," my father said. He spoke in his calm voice, the one he used when he was soothing clients who wanted to cut all their relatives out of their wills. "She's near the top of her class in those. We don't understand about these C's."

Ms. Zero looked down at the paper in the file on her desk.

"Clare has failed to turn in five assignments," she said.

"I turned them in," I said, even though I knew it would do no good.

"You turned them in late."

"No one is saying you can't take marks off for assignments being late," Mom said, "but Clare says you refused to even look at them."

Again, Ms. Zero just nodded.

"She also said she has trouble hearing the assignments sometimes, and when she asks for clarification, you won't give it to her."

More nods.

And a very awkward silence.

"You know from her other teachers that she can do the work," Dad said. "We don't want her average dropping. Do you think you could be a little more flexible?"

"No," Ms. Zero said. "There is no need to be flexible. Clare is capable of doing the assignments and handing them in on time. I run a structured, predictable classroom. Clare, when are homework assignments always given out?"

"The last five minutes of class," I replied, looking down at my nail polish as if I was bored to death by the whole thing.

"And where are they posted after that?"

"On the chalkboard behind your desk."

I deliberately avoided looking at the side chalkboard, where my name was written with "X 12" beside it. No one else had anywhere near that many detentions. The next closest was Brandon, and he only had five. My parents didn't know about any of them.

I kept waiting for Ms. Zero to bring them up. She never did.

"I'm getting the feeling that you don't appreciate our daughter," Mom said.

"Whether or not I appreciate your daughter is immaterial to her grade," Ms. Zero said, "but you're right. She has a good mind and all the tools she needs to turn herself into a fine student. But she just doesn't care."

"It's your job to make her care," my mother said.

"I want my students to develop an appreciation for their abilities," the teacher said. "I want them to take pleasure in the power of their minds. When the world throws difficulties their way, they will need to have the confidence to deal with them. A large part of that is taking responsibility for their lives and choices. Right now, Clare chooses not to do that."

"That's harsh," said my father. "Clare is, after all, only thirteen and a half."

"Which means that in four and a half years, she will legally be an adult," Ms. Zero said. "She has a long way to go in a very short space of time. She could do a lot of that growing this year if she put her mind to it."

At that, my mother stood up. My father and I, after a second, stood up with her.

"My daughter's character is not your concern," she said. "Your job is to teach her history and English literature. I'd appreciate it if you would focus on that."

"Thank you for coming in," Ms. Zero said, not rising and not holding out her hand for a round of handshakes. "There are other schools in this city that offer the eighth grade if you think Clare would be better served elsewhere."

I kept waiting for her to bring up the Statement of Agreement with the fake parent signatures on it, but she didn't.

She closed my file and folded her hands on top of her desk.

We were dismissed.

The next morning, my parents gave me the option of changing schools.

"We talked it over," my father said, "and if you want to switch, that would be fine with us. We want you to be comfortable at school."

I didn't want to start at a new place as a new girl

without my crew with me. And I knew that I could not switch homeroom teachers. I had already tried that. I was stuck.

"I'll stay where I am," I said.

"Then you are playing in her courtroom," Mom said. "It's her rules. So smarten up. I don't have time for this."

She snapped her briefcase closed and headed off to court.

"Your teacher is a smart woman," my dad said. "She'll soon realize what a star you are."

Ms. Zero was right about one thing.

I didn't care. Not about history and not about English literature. And not about impressing her.

But my parents started to take notice of me. Those C's were like the spotlights shining down from the watchtowers along the Big Wall. They shone right down on me. My parents started asking about my assignments and putting limits on my social life. News of all the detentions leaked out to other teachers, who started to look at me in a new way.

Even my crew was starting to make plans that didn't include me.

"We knew you had all those poems to copy out," Josie said. "That's why we didn't ask you to go to the movies with us. We were helping you."

I hated Josie. She was such a phony.

And I hated Ms. Zero. That this one teacher, who didn't even know me, could destroy my whole life like this was totally unfair.

After the parent-teacher conference, I decided it was going to be all-out war. I didn't even pretend to be nice anymore.

Seventeen

———

"WE HAVE a problem," Aaron said.

"You think?" asked Simcha.

"The old lady with the knitting. She's put down her wool and is looking over here. Now she is getting up out of her chair and heading for the door."

I got up on the windowsill to watch. The old lady had something wrong with her legs. She staggered rather than walked, holding on to the house walls and anything else she could lean on while she took step after painful-looking step.

"What is all this singing?" she asked, but her wrinkly old face was smiling. Ms. Fahima went over to her and the two women talked quietly, the teacher glancing in the direction of our little house. The smile left the old woman's face, but she put it on again when she talked to the children.

"You are such pretty singers that I am going to sit right down here and listen to you. Would that be all right?"

The little kids thought that would be just great. Ms. Fahima sent a couple of them into the old woman's house to fetch a chair for her, which they did with great excitement. They brought out her knitting, too. It was funny how excited they got about these silly, ordinary things — seeing a cat, carrying a chair for an old lady. I didn't get it.

As they were getting the old lady settled, a Palestinian television truck pulled up. A reporter and her camera operator got out and headed toward Ms. Fahima. Everyone shook hands.

"Terrific," said Aaron. He took out his voice recorder. "Media has shown up. There will be no aggression from us. We remain quiet in the house."

The reporter briefly interviewed Ms. Fahima. Then the camera was pointed at the house.

I had the ridiculous thought that maybe my family would see me on TV and know that I was all right.

The old lady sat and knitted and the children went back to their singing and their lessons. Ms. Fahima regularly called out to Omar, and each time she did, he squirmed and tried to get away from the soldier who was holding him.

"Omar," the teacher called out, "I know you know your multiplication tables, so I want you to recite them along with us. Loud as you can, now."

The children started at one times one and worked their way through to ten times ten. Omar recited with them, loudly. They were pretty good for little kids. I don't think I could have done that when I was their age.

A couple of old men passing by asked the teacher what was going on. They were told, they looked at the house, and they, too, decided to stay. They sat on the curb along the side of the road and applauded when the children got their answers right.

A small group of Bedouin shepherds came through with their flock of sheep. The children laughed and jumped up and petted the animals. The shepherds stayed and the sheep stayed with the shepherds. The reporter interviewed everyone and captured it all on camera.

The little road outside the little house was getting quite crowded.

It got even more crowded when the stone-throwing boys came running by.

"Get out of our way!" the boys yelled, kicking out at the sheep and pushing the little kids aside. "Move! Let us through!"

One of the shepherds took one of them by the arm and said something to him. The boy looked squarely at our little house. He grabbed his friends and huddled with them for a moment. Then they all looked at the house. A couple of them even approached the window and squished their faces up against it for a second.

I was sitting in the window, but these boys, unlike the little ones, were not interested in a cat. They looked beyond me to the telescope and to the soldiers.

They made faces and a rude gesture.

The boys all backed away, bent down, then stood up again. In the next instant, stones hit the house like hail in a storm.

They yelled as they threw the stones. They didn't stop. They all threw and threw and threw.

Some of the little children started to cry. They gathered around their teacher and tried to hide behind her long dress like little chicks around the feathers of their mama chicken. A few of the little kids picked up stones, too, and tried to throw them like the big boys. Their stones landed on sheep more often than on the house.

The noise attracted more people.

Ms. Fahima reined in the little ones who were trying to throw stones. She comforted the ones who were crying. She was like a shepherd guiding them to a safer spot at the far side of the vacant lot.

She left her young students in the charge of a couple of the older people who were there. Then she marched up to one of the teenaged stone-throwers.

"Abdullah Abbas Soudi, what do you think you are doing?"

The teenager looked surprised to hear his name spoken like that. He looked around at his friends as if he was nervous that they might have overheard. Then he spotted the TV camera and got all puffy chested.

"I'm striking back. What do you think I'm doing?"

"Watch your tone with me, young man," Ms. Fahima said. "And drop that stone!"

"Get out of the way," the teenager said. "Go back to your classroom."

"I'm in my classroom," the teacher said. "And I am here with my students, all of whom are far too young to see this sort of thing going on."

"Tell that to the Israelis!" Abdullah shouted. "There are Israeli soldiers in that house, and you are standing here lecturing me. No more lectures! No more time for talking!"

He tried to shake her away but she would not leave. The other boys started to make fun of him, but she shut them up with one look.

"Have you forgotten everything you learned in my classroom?" she asked. "You have all been my students."

"That was a long time ago, Ms. Fahima," Abdullah said. "Those soldiers in there, they killed my father! They killed Ibrahim's brother. They put our uncles in prison."

"*These* soldiers? Are you sure it was *these* soldiers?"

"Does it matter?"

"Of course it matters."

"Well, it doesn't matter to them! We are all the same to them!" Abdullah broke away from Ms. Fahima and slouched against the lightpost. Then he took a cellphone out of his jeans pocket and spoke quietly into it.

Ms. Fahima gathered the rest of the boys to her and talked with them quietly.

After the boys dropped their stones, Ms. Fahima went back to her students. She led them in a recitation of the Desiderata poem. I guess that's where Omar learned it. The kids recited slowly, in the sing-song rhythm little kids use when they recite. They knew the whole thing. Like I said, these were smart kids. They even had hand gestures for the poem. Like, when it goes, *Be on good terms with all persons*, they made like they were shaking hands with someone.

When they got to the part about being a child of the universe, I could tell that was their favorite part because they shouted it out. Instead of saying *You have a right to be here*, they said *WE have a right to be here* and they pumped their little fists in the air.

It was quite a show.

With everything that was going on, no one was remembering to feed the cat.

I left the window and went searching. There might be food I hadn't sniffed out yet. I sniffed around the kitchen cupboards and the bookshelves and ended up in the City of Dreams.

I snuffled along through the junk city, searching for something I could eat, but just turned up a few more toffees and hard candies.

That's when I knocked over a cardboard school and uncovered a photograph.

It was of Omar standing in front of two adults, a man and a woman. The three of them were dressed in what my grandmother would call their Sunday best. They were posed stiffly, smiling for the camera like the family portraits back in the photographer's window in Bethlehem, Pennsylvania.

I picked up the photo with my teeth and took it over to Omar, rocking in a corner by himself. He stopped rocking and looked at the photo.

"Mama," he said. "Papa."

I sat on my haunches and put a paw on his leg. I wanted to comfort him.

Because I knew something that no one else knew.

Omar's parents were not coming back.

Eighteen

———

I KNEW because I saw the whole thing happen.

It happened at the hole in the wall they call the checkpoint. There's more than one of these spots. Some are big and are often choked up with cars, trucks, vans and buses. Others are small and get choked up with people. They remind me of the border between the United States and Canada, which I crossed with my parents on one of our boring family vacations.

I was there because there are often young soldiers at the checkpoints. Some of them are homesick and they like cats, especially one as friendly as me. I go to the checkpoints and purr and let the soldiers pet me and I chase a rolled-up bit of paper around the floor of the room where they search people, and that makes them laugh. And sometimes they feed me.

This thing with Omar's parents happened at that small crossing place just before I got chased by the cats and came to stay in the little house on the hill. I was quite happy, perched on a post, looking down at the world, hoping for a nice dinner if the soldiers took a break. The two soldiers were both young. And they both liked me.

The crossing was open, but not many people were coming through. It was pretty late at night.

I was nice and relaxed and hoping for supper when a taxi pulled up to one side of the checkpoint, close to the soldiers. A man got out. I could see there was a woman in the back seat, but I couldn't see her well. The man was the same man in the photograph with Omar.

I sniffed and could not smell food on him, so I wasn't too interested. Still, I couldn't help overhearing.

"My wife, she is going to have a baby. We need to get through to the hospital."

"Move your cab back," the soldier said to the cab driver. He gestured with his arms. The taxi started to reverse.

"My wife is in the back!"

The taxi moved back to the place the taxis usually stopped. The man kept looking around wildly, as if he already knew he was trapped.

"Papers, please."

"Papers, yes, yes, papers. They are here." The man started to fumble through his jacket but the young soldier stopped him.

"Why are you wearing that big jacket? Do you have any bags with you? Where are you going?"

"Please let us through," the man said. "My wife is having a baby."

They were talking in two different languages. I understood everything but the soldier and the guy at the checkpoint did not understand. They also were not listening to each other.

A female soldier motioned to the woman to get out of the car. The woman tried, but then she just moaned, a zombie-type moan that I heard on one of those Having My Baby shows on television when I was alive.

"Please get out of the car!" the soldier said again.

Slowly, painfully, the woman swung her legs out of the front seat and, clinging to the door, stood up. She wore the black cloak and head cover some of the women wear on this side of the wall.

"Be careful," the man soldier told the woman soldier. "They send their women over with bombs strapped to them. I lost my cousin to one of them."

The female soldier asked the pregnant woman for her papers. "Where is your identification? Where is your permit to cross this border? Who is your doctor?"

The soldier kept asking her questions in Hebrew. The pregnant woman kept moaning and not answering.

And this is when the circus leapt to a whole new level of craziness. The man — Omar's father — kept saying, in Arabic, "My wife can't hear. She is deaf. Please let us cross!" He motioned to his ears and shook his head. His wife doubled over in pain.

"Tell us who you are!" the man soldier started to yell. "We cannot let you through if you can't prove who you are!"

"Use your radio!" Omar's father said. "Call for one of your ambulances! Do you have a doctor with you here? A medic? A first-aid kit? Please — my wife!"

"She's on the ground," the woman soldier said. She had to talk loudly because of the screams coming from the woman. "I don't know what to do. How do I help her? I can't lift her up!"

"It could be a trick," the man soldier said. "My brother was stabbed by someone pretending to be sick. Back away!"

"My wife!" yelled Omar's father. "Help my wife!"

"Show me your papers! Hey, get back here!"

Omar's father left his own soldier and headed back to the taxi.

"What are you doing?" the man soldier asked. "Get back here!" He shone a very bright flashlight at the taxi. Omar's father, blinded by the light, held his arm up to his eyes.

"My papers are in the cab," he pleaded in Arabic. "I forgot. Let me get them." He opened the back door and reached for something.

"Show me your hands!" the soldier yelled in Hebrew.

The cab driver opened his door, got out and yelled curses at the soldiers.

"Get back in the taxi," the man soldier ordered him.

The cab driver kept standing there and cursing.

Omar's mother screamed one final time, then stopped.

"She's not getting up," the woman soldier yelled. "I can't tell what's going on. She's not moving!"

"Radio for an ambulance," the man soldier told her. "Tell them to hurry!"

There was so much yelling, so many flashlight beams shining in so many different directions. I was scared and I backed up into a shadow.

"Yes, yes, they are here. My papers, they are in this case. I know it's a funny case to keep papers in but it is the only one I have. I've got them right here. I've got my papers."

Omar's father backed out of the taxi. In his hands was something long and black.

"He's got a rifle!"

I heard one shot. And then another.

And then there was silence. A terrible, terrible black silence.

The young soldiers slowly approached the cab. They had their rifles pointed and their flashlights shone over everything. The cab driver was lying in the dirt, not moving.

The man soldier went to Omar's father and knelt down, looking for a pulse. He didn't find one. He picked up the long, black thing they thought was a rifle. It was a violin case. The soldier opened it. He took out a sheaf of papers.

The woman soldier gently shook the pregnant woman, Omar's mother. It was no use.

The two young soldiers looked at each other across the bodies. I could see the tears on both of their faces.

"What happened?" they cried to each other. "What happened?"

The area soon became very busy with ambulances and officials. The bodies were taken away through the checkpoint, the cab was hooked up to a tow truck and hauled to the other side of the wall. There were officers barking orders, investigators taking statements and replacement soldiers beefing up the security.

I waited for quite a while, but nobody brought out any food. So I left. I headed off to sniff out garbage along the high wall, ran into the king tom with the big head, and that's when all of this began.

Nineteen

———

"CONTEXT, CONTEXT, context!"

Ms. Zero wrote the word on the board three times while she said it.

"Context is everything. Understanding the context of something will allow us to understand the meaning of an event, a word, a look, an act. If we don't understand the context, we are liable to misunderstand the details."

I didn't mean to be doodling, but I couldn't take out my new cellphone in class and I had to do something to pass the endless hours of English lit. I started by making one small, innocent circle on the paper. It was followed by another innocent circle.

Then some lines and curves, and before I knew it, I had drawn a very ugly cartoon of my teacher.

"Look at this photograph," she said, putting a large magazine photo on the board. It was a picture of a little girl with curly blonde hair with a big pink bow in it. Most of the photo was covered over. All you could see was a kid's face. "What is your impression of this child? Where do you think she is and what do you think she is doing?"

I only half-listened to the answers.

"She's at a party."

"She's in an ad for pudding."

"She's at Disney World."

Then Ms. Zero uncovered the rest of the photo. "This little girl was in a refugee camp for children orphaned by the violence in Bosnia," she said. "What about this one?"

The second photo was of a little boy with dark skin. He wore a green shirt and camouflage trousers and had a rifle slung over his shoulder.

"Child soldier."

Ms. Zero uncovered the rest of the photo. The little boy was with a bunch of other kids in Hallowe'en costumes.

"Context is everything," she said again. "I want you to write down a scenario where misunderstanding the context could lead to a conflict."

I took the whole context theme and put it into my cartoon. In a frame I put Ms. Zero at a chalkboard. Outside the frame I drew a coven of witches. The context was that Zero looked like an innocent teacher, but really she was a witch, luring children into the black arts.

It was a pretty good bad cartoon, if you know what I mean.

I had a full half second to admire it before Ms. Zero picked it up and looked at it.

"I asked for something in writing," she said, "but I'm

glad to see you understand the concept. Well done."

She handed the cartoon back to me. She didn't get mad and she didn't give me another detention.

It was pretty substantial, my detention total. I had not made one single copy of the poem since the parent-teacher interview. We were now into May. On the board beside my name was the number seventy-five. Some of those were for new crimes. Most were because of the daily accumulation of new ones when the old ones were not turned in.

I had the most detentions of anybody. One kid had five. Another had three. A couple had two. Most kids, when they got detention, copied out the poem and then were done with it.

No one could expect me to copy out that long, stupid poem seventy-five times. No one. And what else could she do to me?

Toward the end of the lesson, Ms. Zero had an announcement.

"The eighth-grade class trip will happen in the second week of June," she said. "We will be going to Washington for five days."

I didn't care about Washington, but it would be fun to be away from home and in a hotel room with my friends. The teachers and chaperones couldn't watch us all the time!

"Permission forms will be available from me tomorrow. Anyone with incomplete assignments will not be able to go. Detentions are considered assignments."

I heard the other kids gasp. It felt like the whole class turned to look at me.

I couldn't quite believe it. My feelings must have shown on my face. A couple of the kids giggled. That just made me madder.

I knew the teacher was daring me to complain, but I was not going to give her that satisfaction.

I would copy the damn poems. And I would enjoy seeing the look on her face when I handed them in.

I used the lunch period to make five copies. I made two more during math class and three more during science. My hand was sore by the end of the day. I half-hoped I was injured, because then my parents could sue her. But then I would have to admit to all the detentions and I wasn't ready to do that yet.

At the end of the day I walked into my homeroom classroom with my ten copies and put them in the center of Ms. Zero's desk. I watched her look them over, then go over to the board and change the number beside my name. She reduced it by ten.

"I'd like a permission form for the trip, please," I said.

Ms. Zero looked at me. "You have made a good start," she said. "When you complete the detentions, then you can have a permission form."

I put on one of my smiles. Not the flashy one, which didn't work with her, but a smaller one. One that I hoped would say, "I'm a really nice girl and I've learned my lesson so please just give me a break."

"It's getting near the end of the year," I started. "There is so much going on right now. Exams, and that big science project. I'm wondering if I could have the rest of the detentions excused."

"If you manage your time well, I think you will find that you can do everything you need to do. The detentions stand."

"I've done ten copies."

"Yes, I've got them. Thank you."

I stood there like a dummy for a full minute.

"That's it?" I asked. "You won't even consider dropping them?"

"I have considered it," she replied. "You just don't like my conclusion. If you do ten copies a day, by the middle of next week, you will be done, and you can place the task behind you."

I stood by her desk in cold silence. We glared at each other for a full minute. Well, I glared. She just looked at me calmly, as if she were watching TV. It made me madder and madder. I wanted to swipe the papers off her desk and kick her chair over. My hands curled themselves into tight fists.

"I hate you," I said.

"You are certainly free to do so. Clare, there are so many long-term benefits you could take away from this detention exercise if you chose to. For example, imagine the sense of accomplishment you will feel when all the copies are completed and you no longer have them hanging over you. And if you actually read the poem while you are copying it out, you will see it is a work of great value. But it is up to you. You will take away from this what you choose."

I turned and walked out of that classroom without saying another word. I stalked down the hallway and, without planning it, found myself at the exit closest to the teachers' parking lot. I walked through that door and stood in front of Ms. Zero's old blue Toyota.

On the ground by my feet was a large rock. I picked it up. It would take nothing to smash in the witch's windshield.

"That would be a criminal act." Ms. Zero had followed me out of the school and was standing behind me. "You know I would report it to the police. Is the momentary satisfaction of breaking my window worth the pain your action would bring upon yourself and your family?"

It almost was. But the anger went out of my shoulders and my arm dropped to my side. The rock hit the dust.

"Excellent choice, Clare. I'm proud of you."

She got in her car and drove away.

I just stood there, in that spot, not knowing what to feel.

I felt strangely proud that Ms. Sealand was proud of me.

And I hated myself for caring what she thought.

Twenty

———

I GOT too sad sitting next to the boy, knowing that his parents were dead and it might be a while before anybody figured it out to tell him. I wanted to forget about him so I went back to the window to see if anything new was going on.

Big mistake. When I got there, Abdullah was standing off to the side, leaning against a lamp post with his hands in his pockets. He was smiling, but I knew it was a mean smile, not a happy smile. While I was watching, he got a call on his cell. It was very short. As soon as he hung up and put the phone back in his pocket, he went to his gang of rock-throwers and got them to move away from the house.

Seconds later, the first bullet hit the house.

It was loud and it was sudden.

In the instant after it hit, the crowd outside the house froze. Then everything and everyone started to panic. The sheep bolted in all directions. The kids screamed and dropped to the ground, covering their heads and rolling up into little balls like those bugs that live in the basement and roll in on themselves when you touch them. The adults tried to cover as many children as they could.

Some of the stone-throwing boys looked scared but excited. Abdullah, who seemed to be the ring-leader, looked defiant. He even looked over at Ms. Fahima and sneered at her the way I used to sneer at Ms. Zero when I made some clever comment about her to my friends.

Inside the house, Omar started rocking back and forth like a rocking horse in a hurricane, wailing the stupid punishment poem at the top of his lungs. Aaron and Simcha had their rifles out. One pointed his gun at the window, the other at the door.

Bang! A second shot hit the house. This one came very close to the door. The third shot came soon after. It hit the door smack at head level.

"I can't see the shooter!" Simcha shouted.

"Are you crazy? Get away from the window!"

The rifle shots excited the stone-throwing boys. They picked up more stones and started heaving them at the house.

Ms. Fahima ran right over to them and pulled on their arms, trying to take the stones away.

"I know all of your parents! I know your teachers and I know your Scout leaders. This is not helping!"

"Out of the way, old woman!" Abdullah said. "If you had done your job right when you were younger and kicked the Israelis out, we would not still be under occupation today!"

"You need to listen," Ms. Fahima said, trying to grab the rock out of Abdullah's hand. He pushed her away. She fell to the ground.

"Hey! Don't push my old teacher!" One of Abdullah's friends knelt down to help her up. Other boys joined him. Ms. Fahima got back to her feet. She was not hurt.

"I'm disappointed in you," she said to Abdullah. "You can make better choices. Think about the long term."

"There is no long term," Abdullah said. "There is no tomorrow. There is only today — and fighting back!"

"I'm going to see if I can see the shooter," Simcha said. "If I can see him, I can get him. Cover me."

"Don't!" shouted Aaron. "You'll make things worse!"

Simcha started to open the door. Omar saw his chance and ran toward the opening. Aaron caught him and put him down on the rug. He put his boot on Omar's back. Not roughly, but with enough pressure to keep the boy there. Omar was a scrawny little thing. It did not take much effort.

Simcha threw open the door and unleashed a volley of bullets from his automatic rifle up in the direction of the sniper fire. Then he backed away and Aaron slammed the door shut.

For a very long moment, everyone played statues.

Then another bullet hit the door.

Nothing had been gained. Everyone was stuck exactly where they were.

The gunfire attracted more attention. The sound of the riots came closer. It was accompanied by the sound of tanks and helicopters and army boots stomping the ground.

"Our guys are here," Simcha said. "About time."

Whatever was going to happen, I would have a front row seat.

Twenty-one

———

WE'RE COMING up to the moment of my death.

I blame a lot of it on my sister.

Polly's handwriting looked a lot like mine. I went to her and asked her to help me write out the punishment poems.

"No," she said.

"Come on! If you don't help me, I won't be able to go on the trip."

"I don't care."

"I'll pay you," I said, even though I didn't have any money, and if I did, I sure wouldn't give it to her.

"I don't need your money," Polly said.

Which, unfortunately, was true. After her furniture store radio commercial, other local businesses hired her, too. She did a radio ad for the health food store and one for Dollar Days, the annual sidewalk sale the downtown business association put on.

"Help me or I'll make your life miserable."

"I'm not afraid of you," she said.

My friends wouldn't help me, either. I wasted lot of time trying to make them.

"You should have done them as you got them," Josie said. "Everybody else did."

I almost hit her.

As the date of the class trip came nearer, I was forced to make a decision. I had to tell my parents about the detentions or I had to do the detentions myself. They already knew about the trip — Polly the rat told them — so they would know something was up if I wasn't on it.

I decided to tell them about the detentions.

"Ms. Sealand has it in for me," I said. "Really, she's been terrible to me all year. I didn't tell you because I wanted to deal with it myself. But she's being really unfair!"

My mother ended up in a meeting with the teacher and the principal during a lunch hour. My father couldn't be there. One of his clients had died and the family was fighting over the will. But I had to attend.

"This is about more than the class trip," my mother said. "I don't care whether Clare goes to Washington with her class or goes with us sometime on a family vacation, or doesn't go at all, for that matter. This is about what appears to be systematic bullying by your teacher of my child."

The principal looked at Ms. Zero.

"You are right that this is about more than the class trip," she said. "The detentions are part of Clare's assignments. If she does not complete them, the incomplete work will bring down her overall average."

"Now, hang on a second," Mom said, getting up on her lawyer legs. "Are you telling me that you might lower my daughter's grades if she doesn't write out some poem you arbitrarily assigned for detention?"

I had a very good feeling about the way the meeting was going, and I was right. The principal did not want a hassle with my mother. He directed Ms. Zero to wipe out the crushing load of punishment poems (he didn't say "crushing load," but that's what it was) and to find another, more reasonable detention for me to do.

Ms. Zero just nodded and said, "All right." She didn't argue. She did not look ashamed. She looked exactly as I imagine she would have looked if she had won.

When I went back to class after lunch, my name was off the board. I got a lot of looks from the other kids, and a lot of questions at recess.

I thought about bragging but I just didn't feel like it.

I think I felt shame. I'm not sure. It's not something I was used to feeling, so I could be wrong.

Twenty-two

_____

AN ARMY helicopter hovered right over the little house.

I heard it come lower. It stirred up dust and blew off people's hats and headscarves. It sent people scurrying into doorways and gutters. There was a volley of machine-gun fire from above.

Were they shooting at the shooters? Nobody told me. There was a lot of shouting but no one seemed to be talking to anyone.

The helicopter rose up again, out of the range of the sniper's rifle fire. That didn't stop all the noise.

My hearing as a cat is very sensitive, something people don't ever think about when they are making loud noises. They never check to see if there is a cat around before they light a firecracker or shoot a gun.

I was small compared to all the people and buildings, but a bullet could easily still find its way to me. I'm sure many cats have been killed in war, not that you ever hear about them on the news. Maybe, if I ever become a human again, I could give speeches in schools about this, and make people more aware of how war is bad for cats.

Some of the boys who had been Ms. Fahima's students helped her round up the little kids and get them and the knitting lady into the old lady's house. They left the kids with the lady and returned to the street.

There seemed to be shots coming from all directions now. I couldn't tell who was shooting. Was the Israeli army shooting at the snipers? Were the snipers trying to kill Aaron and Simcha? Did anyone really know what the heck was going on?

Behind me, Omar wailed with fear and would not shut up. Aaron and Simcha were running around the little house, one moment at the window with their rifles, the next ducking down to take cover. Each time they ducked, they pulled Omar to the ground with them so he would be out of the line of fire. Each time they popped up again, he popped up, too.

I did not want to see him killed.

Some of the people in the streets called out for quiet.

"This demonstration solves nothing!" they said. "Let's calm down and keep everyone safe."

Others called for blood. "Death to Israel! Kill the Jews! Push them into the sea!"

The whole thing was a colossal mess.

One of the rioters brought out a megaphone. He must have been some sort of bigwig rioter because he climbed

up on a rock and the others paid attention to him.

"The Israeli army is holding a Palestinian boy hostage!" he shouted in Arabic. "They have killed his parents at a checkpoint, and now they want to kill him. They won't be happy until every last Palestinian is dead in the streets. We say no more! No more!"

Rioters took up the chant and the noise got worse.

"What did he say?" Simcha asked.

"He said the army killed the boy's parents at a checkpoint," Aaron told him.

Ms. Fahima, with fear all over her face, tried again to open the door.

"Let me inside!" she cried out in Hebrew. "Let Omar go and take me in his place!"

"Do you think it's true?" Simcha asked. "Do you think his parents got killed by our soldiers?"

"If it's true, they'll tear us apart if we go out there," said Aaron. "Get away!" he shouted at Ms. Fahima.

Next came the tear gas, the small black canisters hitting the ground and spewing out bad-smelling fog. Rioters picked up the canisters and threw them back at the Israeli troops, but more kept coming.

The window I was sitting in had a lot of cracks around the windowpane. Cats have a strong sense of smell and tiny lungs. But no one cared about that.

"Back away from the house! Let the soldiers leave and no one will get hurt!" came an order from the army over a loudspeaker.

The rioters ignored it. They started to pound on the door. It was not a strong door. It would not take them very long to break through.

I was thinking of sliding under the sofa to try to stay safe, when a rock broke through the window. I was covered in shattered glass.

In the same instant, some rioter plunged an ax into the door.

They were going to get in. People were going to die.

Twenty-three

———

WHICH BRINGS me to the day I died.

The day my detentions were erased, Ms. Zero asked me to stay behind at the end of school.

I have to admit, I was curious to see what she would do. I swaggered a bit as I walked up to her desk.

She put down her pen, sat back in her chair and looked up at me. She smiled her vampire smile.

"It's been quite a year, hasn't it?" she said.

I didn't reply. She went on talking.

"And it's almost over. I wonder what the takeaway will be for you. When you're an old woman and you look back on your time in the eighth grade, I wonder what you will remember."

She stood up.

"One last detention," she said. "Come with me."

I figured she was going to make me clean out some cupboard or storage room, so I followed her. But she stopped at the classroom door.

Right beside the poster of the punishment poem.

I looked at her.

"I'm not copying it out," I said. "The principal said I didn't have to."

"I don't want you to copy it out," she said. "I just want you to read it. One time. Out loud."

I was sure it was a trick.

"I just read it and then I'm done?"

"That's right," she said.

"You can't make me read it."

"You are correct," she said. "I am asking you to read it. You can choose to do it or not. But I can't imagine why you wouldn't. It's simple enough."

I stared at her. Then I stared at the poster. My fingers started to curl into fists.

"Tell you what," she said. "I'll read it with you. We'll alternate verses. I'll start us off. *Go placidly amid the noise and the haste and remember what peace there may be in silence.*"

She looked at me and waited. I wanted to smash her.

Instead, I read the next line. No, that's not true. I didn't read it. I recited it. Somehow, the poem had worked its way into my brain even though I did not want it there.

"*As far as possible, without surrender, be on good terms with all persons.*"

"*Speak your truth quietly and clearly; and listen to others, even to the dull and the ignorant; they too have their story,*" said Ms. Zero. She wasn't reading, either.

"If you compare yourself with others, you may become vain or bitter," I spat out. My voice got louder. *"... for always there will be greater and lesser persons than yourself."*

"Be yourself," Zero said calmly.

"Take kindly the counsel of the years ..." You old cow, I thought.

"Many fears are born of fatigue and loneliness."

"... be gentle with yourself," I said. The damn thing was almost over. My eyes were starting to sting.

Ms. Sealand took a step toward me. Her face looked kind and concerned. She looked the way my grandmother looked when some ratty old, smelly old drunk came into the soup kitchen in the winter without shoes.

"You are a child of the universe," she said, putting her hand gently on my arm. *"... no less than the trees and the stars; you have a right to be here."*

I backed away. *"And whether or not it is clear to you ..."*

I knew the rest of the words in that line. Of course I knew them. They just wouldn't come out of my mouth.

I felt a tear dripping down my cheek. Ms. Zero wasn't exactly blocking the door, but she wasn't making it easy for me to run through it, either.

I wasn't going to let her win. I wiped my cheek with the back of my hand and tried again.

"And whether or not it is clear to you ..."

Ms. Zero finished the line for me.

"... no doubt the universe is unfolding as it should."

That was it. I'd had enough.

I pushed my way passed Zero and out into the empty hall. I swung out at open locker doors and kicked a stray gym shoe out of my way.

Stupid school, I thought. Stupid poem. The universe was *not* unfolding as it should. The universe was a big freaking mess where good people got killed and where people like me were able to keep on living.

I went to my locker and I gathered up all my stuff. I was finished with that school and I was finished with Ms. Zero. I didn't know what kind of lie I'd tell my parents to keep from having to go back, but I'd figure something out. I was going to walk out of that school and never walk back into it again.

Which is exactly what happened.

Loaded down with binders, gym bag, books and jackets, I took out my phone and texted mean things about Ms. Zero as I left the school.

I kept sending messages when I got outside, messages slamming her stupid lectures and her ugly smile and the way she dressed like a prison guard. I walked fast, wanting to get far away from that terrible school and all the people in it.

I approached the street. I kept walking, texting furiously with every step.

Ms. Zero was standing across the street, talking with some dumb student from the sixth grade. I saw her look up and see me.

And she started to wave.

She was waving at me to cross over to her.

Stupid poem, I texted as I stepped out into the road. *Stupid poem from a stupid teacher.*

And that's when the truck hit me.

And that's when I died.

It was all her fault. She waved me over. She killed me.

Twenty-four

———

"GET AWAY from the door or we will shoot!"

The order from the military loudspeaker boomed through the air.

"Death to Israel!" the rioters chanted. "Smash the occupation!"

I was afraid to move. I was covered in window glass. If I got a piece of glass stuck in my paw, I would not be able to get it out, and even if I did, the wound could get infected. But I had to move because the rioters were excited by the danger and the sound of things breaking. They could burst into the house and crush me.

"We have to get out of here," Simcha said. "Put the boy in front. If they see him first, they might not attack us."

"We're not using a child as a shield," said Aaron. "That's not who we are. We'll put him between us. They're crazy out there. We have to protect him."

"Either we go out or they're coming in. Out there, at least we've got the army to back us."

Aaron tried to grab Omar. Omar pulled away and ran over to me. He quickly brushed the glass from my fur, cutting his fingers but not stopping. I stood still and let him do it. When he had the biggest pieces gone he picked me up and held me against his chest, tight in his arms. He carried me to the door.

"Goplacidlyamidthenoiseandthehaste ..." he said as Simcha opened the door. I said the words with him.

Aaron moved the boy and me behind him and in front of Simcha. We stood in the open doorway for a moment and let everyone get a good look at us.

The Israeli army moved forward. The rioters moved forward.

"Back off!" warned the army over the loudspeaker.

"You back off!" the crowd yelled back.

A weird silence fell on the area like a fog. I saw soldiers aim their rifles. I saw teenaged boys pick up rocks.

It looked like all hell was going to break out right over us.

And that's when I made my move.

I did it without thinking. I just did it.

I leapt down from the boy's arms and out into the little space between the enemies.

I started to dance.

I danced for all of them, up on my hind legs.

I jumped. I twisted in the air. I pretended to catch a bird and I batted around an invisible mouse. I flopped on my back and waved my paws. I strutted and boogied and made myself look like a complete and utter idiot.

And everybody shut up and stopped to watch.

Soldiers lowered their rifles and rioters dropped their rocks.

"What's with the cat?" I heard someone say.

That was just enough.

Everyone took a breath. Ms. Fahima came over and took Omar into her arms. The soldiers grabbed Aaron and Simcha and took them out of the way of the rioters. Everyone went back to their corners.

My performance knocked the wind right out of their sails, as my grandmother would say.

Everyone drifted away from the little house. The soldiers went back to their base. The villagers went home. Omar went with Ms. Fahima.

And I was left all alone.

Twenty-five

——

AFTER EVERYONE had left and I was alone, it turned into an ordinary day. I had to sniff around the garbage bags for food. I had to avoid the other cats. I had to be careful not to get run over when I crossed the road.

No one thanked me. No one even remembered that I was there.

I was alone again, and no one cared.

It's the sort of thing that should make me feel very sorry for myself. And I've tried. I've tried to go back to my old thoughts, my blaming-Ms.-Zero-for-everything thoughts, but it's not working.

I did something useful, even though it was a very small thing. It wasn't like I brought peace to the world or anything. I just kept some people from killing each other for a little while. I was useful. It felt good.

Nothing I did will last. Omar will live the rest of his life without his parents. The killing will keep on going.

But in that little place, for those little moments, I actually did something good.

Context is everything, Ms. Sealand said. Without understanding context, we are going to keep getting things wrong.

I think I got something wrong about her.

She may not have hated me. She may not have had it in for me from the beginning.

She may not have been waving to get me to cross the street.

She may have been waving to tell me to stay where I was.

I don't know what the point is of this new understanding. I can't do anything with it. I can't repeat the eighth grade and do it the way I should have done it the first time. I can't go back and tell Polly I'm sorry for calling her Fishface. I'll never play Monopoly again on a Family Game Night. That's all passed for me.

Unless this *is* all a coma, and I'm going to wake up and get my life back. Or unless God decides I've done my detention as a cat, moves me up to heaven and lets me see my grandma again.

I don't know what's going to happen. Nobody ever tells me anything.

I can't keep wandering around eating garbage and running from other cats. All this thinking has messed with my head and I'm really missing my family.

I need to have a plan.

I think I'll go look for Omar. He can't be that hard to find. Maybe he'll remember me. Maybe he'll let me be his new family.

Maybe the world is not completely rotten.

Maybe I'll strive to be happy.

ABOUT THE AUTHOR

Deborah Ellis is the celebrated author of more than twenty books for young people. She is best known for her Breadwinner series, which has been published in twenty-five languages and has earned more than $1 million in royalties to benefit Canadian Women for Women in Afghanistan and Street Kids International. She has won the Jane Addams Children's Book Award, the University of California's Middle East Book Award, the Governor General's Award, the Ruth Schwartz Award, Sweden's Peter Pan Prize and the Vicky Metcalf Award for a Body of Work. She recently received the Ontario Library Association's President's Award for Exceptional Achievement, and she has been named to the Order of Ontario. She lives in Simcoe, Ontario.

A CONVERSATION WITH DEBORAH ELLIS

by Jennifer Abel Kovitz

Photo credit: Heidy van Dyk

Q: You've said that you wrote *The Cat at the Wall* after returning from your second trip to Israel-Palestine and feeling more confused than before you left, and that the novel is your "attempt to sort it all out." Can you elaborate on what you mean by this?

A: The first time I went to Israel and Palestine, late in 2002, I came home thinking the conflict was primarily due to the two sides not knowing one another. The children had very few, if any, opportunities to interact with each other. Consequently, their knowledge of the other side was limited to news reports and violent encounters. This made it difficult for them to see the humanity of the other side.

Ten years later, the two groups are even more divided. I have learned — through countless conversations with many people who have very different perspectives — that the situation is hugely complicated. Instead of just Israelis and Palestinians, there are many groups and many complex points of view. It often can feel as though the power of the individual to make a difference can get lost in the complexity of the world. *The Cat at the Wall* tries to figure out a place for individual choice in the face of big events.

Q: Fans of your Breadwinner series and your novel *No Ordinary Day* will find *The Cat at the Wall* an innovative departure from your past methods of weaving a memorable tale. In this new story, the narrator, Clare, once a thirteen-year-old girl, finds herself reincarnated as a stray cat in the West Bank. Did you always imagine the novel from this creative perspective, or did Clare's unique situation develop over several drafts?

A: The prompt for this novel was learning from former Israeli soldiers about the "Straw Widow" operations, wherein Israeli soldiers take over the home of a Palestinian family and use it to spy on the neighborhood. The family is usually in the home at the time, made to remain quietly in one room, sometimes for days. Israeli soldiers tell of families who have been through this a few times. They offer the soldiers coffee and discuss football matches. The whole thing is fascinating — how everyone relates to each other in a very enclosed, very loaded situation. It got me wondering how it all might play out. I wanted to be a fly on the wall in one of these situations, but thought that a cat would be just as good as an interloper. But I didn't want to write in the voice of a cat. That's how Clare came into the picture.

Q: In 2004, you released *Three Wishes: Palestinian and Israeli Children Speak*, a collection of interviews. Are there threads of themes or voices from this collection that readers will recognize in *The Cat at the Wall*?

A: In *Three Wishes*, over and over we meet good, kind-hearted people who do not know the other side. It is easy enough for us to get things wrong when we are communicating with people who share our own culture, history, language and situation. So it is easier still to get things wrong when we speak through a fog of differences. By trying to clear away that fog and find out what we have in common, we can have a better chance of not misunderstanding each other.

Q: Tell us a bit about the two Israeli soldiers in the novel. Simcha is a somewhat over-zealous American Jewish transplant, while Aaron seems to resist seeing the world as "good versus bad." Both soldiers are rather young themselves, barely out of their teenage years. What kind of research did you do to bring these two characters to life? What is their role in the story?

A: One of the lessons I have had to learn over and over in my life is that every group is made up of individuals, and those individuals each have their own motives and ways of interpreting the world. I was reminded of that when I was writing my books on Afghanistan and also when I wrote *Off to War*, a book of interviews with North American military families.

When I was writing *The Cat at the Wall*, I thought about what it might be like to be a soldier in this situation — young, away from home, stationed in a place that has always seemed like foreign or enemy territory, trying to make good while still in the midst of forming themselves into the people they want to be. The two soldiers in the book, Simcha and Aaron, act quite naturally out of fear on occasion, but they also make deliberate choices that affect the outcome of the story.

Q: Where do you find hope for reconciliation and peace in the West Bank?

A: It is so easy to look at the Middle East and see only a colossal mess with people firmly entrenched in their versions of the story and with powerful forces benefiting from keeping the conflict alive. Look a bit closer, and we find a host of smart, kind, strong, forward-thinking women and men who are reaching beyond old hatreds and habits to create a new destiny for themselves and those around them.

Q: You speak to young people in middle schools across North America. Did these school visits influence how you wrote about the conflicts in Israel and Palestine? What have you learned during these visits that helps you better write conflict in language that middle-grade readers can understand?

A: I've been doing school visits since 1999, when my first book, *Looking for X*, was published. It is a huge privilege to be invited into schools and meet with kids who are learning how to figure out the world around them. When I'm writing, my main goal is to try to understand a situation better myself. I generally don't think about the audience. If kids read and like my books, I think it is because they — like all of us — are attracted to courage. I get to write about incredibly brave people from all around the world.

Q: You first engaged with political activism as a teenager. What were the early causes that inspired you to action? How might educators and parents encourage young people today to take a stand and change the world for the better?

A: I first got engaged in political activism in the late 1970s, when I was a teenager campaigning against atomic weapons. That led me into women's rights and work for social justice. And we learn so much through the examples of others. My parents were not involved in politics but they were always volunteering in the community, stocking shelves at the food bank, planning activities in old-age homes, taking Alzheimer's patients on outings, or gardening for a sick neighbor. They taught me that we can contribute to one another and that these small actions build a better community.

Q: Your commitment to issues of social justice and disenfranchisement permeates many facets of your work, including the money you earn for the twenty-plus books you have written (you donate most of your royalty income). To which organizations do you donate, and what about their missions inspires you?

A: I'm a terrible fundraiser and a lousy organizer, so I'm grateful to be able to contribute to some terrific organizations through the sale of my books. The International Board on Books for Young People (IBBY) has a Children in Crisis fund that sends books to kids in war zones. Canadian Women for Women in Afghanistan works with grassroots women's groups in Afghanistan to build schools, train female teachers, put libraries into communities, assist women to start income-generating projects and more. The Leprosy Mission Canada works with people affected by leprosy around the world, getting drugs to those still infected with the disease and working with them afterwards to ensure they have lives of dignity and productivity. Money from my books about AIDS goes to UNICEF, to further girls' education globally.

Visit Deborah Ellis's website, deborahellis.com, and find her on Twitter @DebEllisAuthor.